PARAMOUR

PARAMOUR

by

Margaret Ethridge

Allison -
Thanks so much for all
of your support!
Margaret Ethridge

Turquoise Morning Press
Turquoise Morning, LLC
www.turquoisemorningpress.com

Turquoise Morning, LLC
P.O. Box 43958
Louisville, KY 40253-0958

Paramour
Copyright © 2011, Margaret Ethridge
Print ISBN: 9781935817376

Cover Art Design by Kim Jacobs

Electronic release, January, 2011
Trade Paperback release, January, 2011

Acknowledgements

Many, many thanks to Kim and Jennifer at Turquoise Morning Press. Their enthusiasm and guidance have made this experience truly exhilarating.

I waited a long time for my happily ever after, but I'm living it with my husband, Bill. Not only is he a wonderful husband and amazing father, but he also happens to be the love of my life. Thank you for putting up with my madness. I am a very lucky woman.

I want to thank my kids, Joey and Arron, who have consumed enough Sonic Drive-In meals to turn into tater tots; my mother, Suzanne, for raising a family of readers; and my siblings, nieces, and nephews for administering equal amounts of abuse and encouragement.

Big wet smooches to the Super Cool Party People. You have changed my life irrevocably. You're my bedrock, my inspiration, and my joy, and my life *would* suck without you.

Thank you to my critique partner, Joyce, for her invaluable feedback and unflagging enthusiasm.

This book is dedicated to my Head Cheerio, Julie Doner.

Julie is my punctuation queen, sounding board, and partner in crime. She also makes me smile every single day. She cracks the whip when I'm feeling sluggish, and allows me to bask in her eternal positivity when I'm running on empty. Thanks, Jewels. You truly are the best!

Thank you all for helping make this dream come true.

PARAMOUR

*Two men: one living, one dead,
and both vying for her love.*

Camellia Stafford has never been alone in her room. For twenty years, she's been engaged in a fierce power struggle with her bedroom's previous tenant, Frank DeLuca, the ghost trapped in the light fixture above her bed.

Caustic and cranky, Frank has one soft spot—Cam. Over the years, their feelings for one another have evolved from grudging friendship to an enduring love that burns white-hot until Frank puts his feelings for Cam on ice.

When she suffers the loss of her beloved father, Cam returns home to say good-bye, and confront her feelings for Frank. She finds an unexpected shoulder to lean on in neighbor, Bradley Mitchum. Cam falls hard and fast for the handsome ad man's charming smile and passionate nature, but Brad's easy-going exterior masks a steely backbone tempered by adversity.

Now Cam must choose— Is her heart strong enough to determine which dream could lead to a love that will last a lifetime?

Prologue

I break everything I touch.

That's what my mother always told me. She thought the whole, *See, Frankie? This is why we can't have nice things,* bit was invented with me in mind. I don't think I was a particularly destructive kid—I was just a normal boy.

Stepping into the room, I pitch my voice at a whisper so I don't startle her. "Mom?"

She doesn't answer. She sits frozen on the edge of my old bed. Her hands are folded in her lap, her legs crossed at the ankles. Her long, graceful fingers coil into her palm. I open my mouth to speak, but no words come out.

I want to tell her I'm okay, by some miracle I'm alive, but the words gurgle in my throat, trapped in my chest. I glance down. The shirt I wore earlier has been cut away. I blink to clear my vision, stunned to find only the faintest smears of dried blood on my skin. And a hole. A hole no bigger than a dime.

I raise my hand. The metal studs on my leather wrist band flash in the light from the cone-shaped sconce on the wall above my bed. I press my fingers to the hole, hoping I can muffle the faint sucking that should have been my breath.

It doesn't work.

The hole is empty, dark, and fathomless, burrowing straight through me. I bend my arm and grope at my back. My own blood chokes me when I touch the ragged edges of a much larger void. There had been no miracle. I'm not okay.

I grasp the closet doorknob and yank. Empty wire hangers rattle and clatter on the rod, but still she doesn't stir. My fingers close around something soft, and I pull with all my strength, needing to prove I have some strength left.

My prize is a faded Metallica concert tee shirt I snagged at the Goodwill Store the summer I turned seventeen. The summer I let her down. I don't care if the shirt is two sizes too small. I don't care if the album the tour supported sucked. I don't care about anything but covering the empty spot where my heart once beat.

The hem of the shirt barely skims the top of my 501s, and the sleeves choke my arms. I tug at one, but then figure it doesn't matter. She'd never let me be buried in this anyway. I take a step closer to the bed, trying to sneak a peek at her face.

Stoic. I know that face well. She wore the same look when she poured me bowlfuls of Count Chocula in the mornings. The same mornings we pretended her eye wasn't swelling shut.

Silent. She stares at the wall, not uttering a word. My mother remains clammed up like she was on the nights my father would stumble home sober enough to give her a good beating.

Stone-faced. Her fine features tight and chiseled, like she's carved from granite. Mary Katherine DeLuca never showed any emotion. Years of living under the threat of Big Frank's fists taught her well.

I guess the silence held her together the night Dad's buddies from the Force came to tell her that her husband was dead. I suppose the stoicism is what kept her from rushing down to the lock-up to thank the punk whose convenience store robbery my father had interrupted.

But the stony planes of her cheekbones cut me now. I hate her and her stony, silent stoicism.

She doesn't appear surprised I had somehow managed to break my life. I guess I still can't help it. Breaking things seems to be my fate.

Still, I ached. *I'd* never hurt her. At least, not with my fists. I wanted to believe deep inside she knew I never would. I'm sure it had to be pretty deep because from the time I'd grown taller than Big Frank, I'd catch her flinching if I moved too fast. I stopped touching her long before my father did. I didn't want to be the one who made her jump like a frightened rabbit.

I hurt her in other ways.

I couldn't be what she wanted me to be. Lord knows, I tried. I swear I did, but school bored me to tears. I couldn't imagine ever facing the pressing need to diagram a sentence, employ the Pythagorean Theorem, or recite the Gettysburg Address.

The only thing I ever found useful was Mr. Williams' shop class. There, I learned how to break things down and build them up again, using my own two hands. I'm good with my hands. So good that Rusty Matteson offered me a part-time job at his restoration shop.

My mother hoped it was a passing phase. She made comment after comment about boys and their obsession with cars. She'd hum *Greased Lightning* under her breath while I'd stand at the kitchen sink, scrubbing my nails with a bar of Lava and a brush. I played along, counting the days until August.

My eighteenth birthday was three days after my senior year of high school started. I put in those three days, kissed Warrenton High goodbye, and never looked back. My mother was stunned. She never dreamed I wouldn't finish. She didn't care about my dreams. She only wanted me to live the life she dreamed for me.

Moving closer, I kneel beside the bed. My hand hovers over her knee. She doesn't flinch, but she doesn't reach for me either. That hits me harder than the bullet.

My hand falls away, clutching at the too-tight shirt, stretching the cotton away from my skin. There are things I need to say to her. There are things I need her to hear. I'm scared. I need her. I need her like I haven't needed her since I was a little boy.

I want her to brush my hair back from my forehead. I need the whisper of her breath as she tells me to hush, and the caress of her hand when she promises everything will be okay.

"Mom," I croak, fighting past the bubble in my throat.

I raise my hand and touch her knee. No response. She just sits and stares. Tearless, unflinching, stoic—like I'm no better than my father, and she's not surprised.

I start to pull away, but she stands. The abrupt movement knocks me back. She takes two steps and snatches the tallest trophy from the top of my bookshelf. It's the MVP trophy from my last year of Junior League baseball. The summer after my father died. The summer I thought we'd both finally be free.

The trophy is spotless, gleaming bright gold in the light cast from the cheesy 70s directional sconce mounted on the wall. She runs her fingertip over the engraved plate bearing my name, Francis DeLuca.

Her fingers close around the tiny gilt batter on top. I roll to my feet when she starts into her wind-up.

A scream rips from her throat, and I flinch as she hurls the trophy across the room.

My last breath, the one I've been clinging to so desperately, seeps from my lungs. The trophy hits the light, shattering the bulb into a million pieces.

It's disappearing. I'm disappearing. The darkness draws me away from the safety of her embrace, into what had moments before been a circle of light.

On August nineteenth, nineteen-eighty-seven, I died.

She broke. I broke her. I didn't think it was possible. My whole life, I thought she was indestructible. But she's not. She's broken, and I broke her. My mother crumpled in a heap on the floor. For a moment, I was happy. I finally got a rise out of her.

Chapter One

The brakes on Camellia Stafford's battered, old Chevy protested her neglect with a squeal. She jerked to a stop in the driveway behind her father's Buick. Warm and snug in the car's musty interior, she listened to the hiss of the spring drizzle coating the windows. The rain suited her mood, falling in tiny drops so cold they almost bounced off the windshield but still clung to the glass in a shimmering veil of tears.

Cam's eyes blurred. Exhaustion distorted perception until the edges of the world ran together like the raindrops.

Someone tapped on the window. Cam jumped, rapping her knuckles on the gear shift. She blinked at the bright yellow blob hovering at the driver's door. Her brain clicked into gear when she spotted the familiar blue flowers of a vintage Corning Ware casserole dish. She reached for the door handle and began to unfold herself from the driver's seat.

"Hi, Mrs. Kelly."

"Camellia, Bob and I are so sorry," her father's next-door neighbor said in a rush. She thrust the casserole dish into Cam's hands and pulled the hood of her yellow rain slicker tighter around her carefully coiffed hair. "We're stunned. Your father always seemed in such good health."

Cam attempted a smile, but a creaking sensation in her cheekbones stopped her. "Thank you, Mrs. Kelly." She managed to eke the words out around the tears clogging her throat.

With a sorrowful shake of her head, Mrs. Kelly tapped the lid with one gnarled finger. "Now, that's tuna noodle. Just put the dish in the oven at three-fifty degrees for about thirty minutes."

The older woman's brisk instructions did the trick. A corner of Cam's mouth lifted, and she nodded.

"Or you can freeze the whole shebang if you don't want it right away," Mrs. Kelly continued.

Certain another full set of instructions on safe food storage procedures would soon follow, Cam shook her head. "No. This is perfect. A cold, rainy night needs tuna noodle casserole."

"Do you want me to make you some cornbread? Bob always likes fresh-baked cornbread with a casserole."

"No. Thank you." Cam hefted the dish. "This is more than enough. Way more than enough for just me."

The old woman gasped and pressed her swollen knuckles to her lips.

"I didn't think!" In a flash, her bony fingers gripped Cam's arm. "You can't stay here all alone," she implored. "Come home with me. We'd love to have you. You can stay in Veronica's room."

Cam's eyes widened. "Oh! No, Mrs. Kelly!"

Her heart began to hammer as she tried to envision herself sleeping in Veronica Kelly's girlhood room. Dozens of creepy Madame Alexander dolls would stare at her. She knew she definitely wouldn't sleep a wink. Veronica had escaped their glassy-eyed stares, but only because she married a man who spent his formative years smashing mailboxes with a baseball bat.

"No, really. Thank you. I have... I have calls to make. You understand..." Cam attempted another smile with only a slightly better result.

"Of course. Is there anything I can help you with, dear?"

The sincerity in Mrs. Kelly's voice coated Cam's frayed nerves like a balm. The creak in her cheekbones eased, and her smile came more easily.

"Thank you, but no. I'll be fine. You should go inside. It's a nasty day out here." Turning toward her father's house, Cam clutched the casserole dish like a talisman. "Thank you for dinner."

"Don't worry about the dish," Mrs. Kelly called after her. "I wrote our name on a piece of tape and stuck it to the bottom. I'll pick it up next week."

Cam waved and stabbed at the lock with her key. Safely inside the dim foyer, she leaned against the door. A grimace curled her lip as she stared at the congealed beige sludge trapped under the clear glass lid. She sighed and carried the dish into the kitchen.

Wandering into the living room, she tried to make sense of the day's events. She'd been out of coffee that morning. When she was on a deadline, groceries were usually the first chore she dropped. The article she sold to a travel magazine seemed to write itself. Her recent trip to Mexico had gone off without a hitch.

Cam bit her lip, refusing to think about the silver money clip she had picked out for her father while in Cozumel. She didn't want to remember the phone call that interrupted the flow of her article, or the news it brought. She couldn't bear to relive the moment when she burst through the hospital doors, only to find her father's business partner slumped in a plastic chair, shaken and grim.

The rest of the day passed in a blur. She didn't think; she acted. She made decisions. Arrangements were arranged. Her father was gone, and now she was all alone.

The silence of the house closed in on her, loneliness thrumming like a bass, low and deep inside of her. She moved through the room. Her fingers trailed over an octagonal end table, unable to stir even a speck of dust. She envisioned her father wielding his battered feather duster, and a sad smile played at her lips.

Twenty-four hours ago, he'd been alive and preparing for the week ahead. He did his *inside chores* on Sunday mornings. Just yesterday, he had dusted, vacuumed, and straightened. Today he was dead.

Cam spun on her heel and hurried back to the kitchen. She snagged the casserole from the counter and attempted to shove the dish into the already packed freezer. Bricks of hamburger squished into quart-sized freezer bags tried to thwart her advances. Row after row of pint containers filled with garden vegetables served as fortification. As if united, they repulsed the invasion of the cornflower blue stenciled ceramic.

With a distinctly unladylike grunt, Cam surrendered. Her fingers unfurled just enough to allow the smooth handles to slip from her grasp.

She gasped as the casserole fell in slow motion. Noodles separated from the cream-of-mushroom-clad tuna, but somehow combined forces to jettison the heavy glass lid. The dish itself landed on her toes, spattering her jeans and the refrigerator with milky chunks of albacore.

"Gah!"

Pain speared through her foot, and the glass lid came to rest against the baseboard. Hopping on one foot, Cam shook her leg in an attempt to dislodge the slippery bits of mushroom, pasta, and fish. She snatched the dishcloth from the lip of the sink and wiped ineffectually at the clotted casserole that clung to her jeans.

A wide strip of masking tape with 'KELLY' written in neat block letters stuck to the bottom of the dish. Something in her brain clicked, and she paused to question the wisdom of putting masking tape into a three hundred and fifty degree oven for thirty minutes.

Cam tossed the towel into the sink and slid the pointed toe of her boot out from under the oozing dish. Biting her lip hard, she blinked away the burn of tears. Her heartbeat rushed in her ears. The air was still, thick with unshed tears and the silence of too many unanswered questions.

The freezer door swung shut when she backed away. She turned to the window and stared out at the backyard.

Burgeoning leaves trembled in the late spring wind. In each of the far back corners of the yard, a scraggly, overgrown camellia bush dwarfed the fence. They'd been planted in honor of the first two birthdays she'd celebrated in this house, and neglected by a man who lost all reason to celebrate the following year.

Hot, fresh tears filled her eyes. Plump droplets gathered on her lashes. Cam closed her eyes and focused on their warmth as they slithered down her cheeks. The tears plinked into the sink, dull and soft, losing their strength when they struck scrubbed stainless steel.

Cam swiped impatiently at her cheeks and pushed away from the sink to stumble into the living room. She nudged aside the heavy drapes swagging the picture window and focused on the pristine front yard.

Flowerbeds braced the front of the house and reinforced the low white picket fence. Neatly trimmed hedges anchored beds filled with evenly raked hardwood mulch, but they weren't the focal point. No, the glory of those flowerbeds was poised in the tentative shoots of green that broke through the ground at precise twelve inch intervals.

Daylilies, tiger lilies, stargazers, trumpets, hybrids, Oriental and Asiatic. Soon rare, exotic lilies with names she couldn't pronounce would pop up. Easter lilies planted from years before would grant encore performances. Bulbs of untested origin would be imported in the hope that they too would flourish.

Despite the long hours he toiled at his accounting business, everyone who knew him knew these beds were Jim Stafford's heart. Petted and cosseted, her father's lilies would thrive and survive here—unlike the neglected camellias in the backyard and unlike her mother, Lily Stafford.

Cam backed away from the window, rushing through the room and down the hall. She stopped in the doorway to the room at the far end and peered into the gloom. The IBM Selectric typewriter sat at the center of the neat desk, its dustcover pristine.

Her fingers slid from the casing of her mother's office door. With her feet planted firmly in the hall, she leaned in to grasp the cut glass doorknob. Unused brass hinges protested loudly when she pulled the door closed. The sound of the latch catching for the first time in twenty years echoed in the emptiness.

She fled into the comfortable security of the room across the hall. Her room.

Heedless of her stained jeans, she fell face-first onto the narrow single bed. She wrapped her arms around a pillow stuffed into a faded rose-printed cotton sham. Inhaling deeply, she picked up the scent of Cheer detergent and searched for a hint of Love's Baby Soft that used to linger in the room.

A tinge of something different tickled her nostrils. The heady, familiar aroma made the tiny hairs on the back of her neck stand at attention. The tantalizing fragrance wasn't a trace of her father's traditional splash of Old Spice. She raised her head, and her nostrils twitched as she tried to pick up the thread once more, but it was gone, drifting away like a memory.

Cam groaned her frustration and flipped onto her back to stare at the popcorn ceiling. She cataloged the familiar peaks and valleys while she ran through the list of things she'd need to accomplish in the next few days.

The silence hummed around her. Her stomach growled as if to chastise her for the casserole wasted on the kitchen floor. She rubbed the edge of her thumbnail over the pad of her index finger. When fidgeting didn't prove effective, Cam pressed her hand over her heart and carefully measured the strength of each beat against her fingertips.

She told herself everything would be okay. Here in her room, she was safe. Her eyelashes fluttered with the herculean effort it took to open them.

Cam reached up and twisted the tiny stem on the cone-shaped reading lamp above her bed. A beam of light swept the length of the bed, bathing the faded comforter in a warm, golden glow.

Cam basked in the soothing pool of light, safe in her girlhood room. She studied the rosebud-patterned wallpaper and silently thanked her mother for being too bohemian to collect Madam Alexander dolls. The silence throbbed like an ache. She closed her eyes and wished she could hear her father's tuneless humming just one more time.

She didn't stir when the edge of her bed dipped. Instead she held her breath for a moment before opening her eyes. Francis John DeLuca sat perched on the edge of the mattress.

She stared at him, drinking in the little details. She knew the leather bracelet he wore had sixteen rows of studs. The ends of the strip of coarse black hair he wore in a Mohawk curled ever so slightly. A tiny gold hoop in his ear gleamed in the light and a Metallica shirt stretched taut across his shoulders. The sleeves cut into his biceps, but the fabric made no indention in his smooth olive skin.

The scent was back, flooding her senses with the relief of homecoming.

She wondered if he knew how many hours she'd spent at the men's cologne counter sniffing samples, trying to place the fragrance. After twenty years of friendship, endless fights, and one unforgettable kiss, she'd wondered if she finally earned the right to ask questions.

"Are you really here?" she whispered, afraid she'd scare him away.

"Yeah."

Their eyes met, and she tumbled into the depths of his dark gaze. Cam knew if she didn't take the chance this time, she may never have another.

"What cologne do you wear?"

Frank's eyes narrowed with typical caution. "Polo."

"Huh. Smells different on you."

His thick eyebrows rose, and a sardonic smile twitched his lips. "Might be because I'm dead."

Cam swallowed hard and sat up. "I'm glad you're here."

"Welcome home. I'm sorry."

She shook her head, forcing a small, flirtatious smile. "Did you miss me?"

"Every damn day."

"Then don't leave me again."

Frank raised his hand. His fingers twitched. She could feel heat radiating from his palm. Those warm fingers curved along the contour of her cheek.

"I'll make sure you're never alone."

Cam smiled, smoothing her palm over the rough hairs on the back of his hand. "With you around, how could I be?"

She stretched out once again and closed her eyes, certain he'd stay perched on the edge of her bed watching over her as she slept. Cam drifted off, secure in the knowledge that she would never truly be alone in her room.

****

Frank chuckled when she smacked her lips and rolled onto her side. Cam snuggled deep into the pillow. A part of him envied her ability to sleep. She always gave herself over to dreams without reservation. It shouldn't surprise him; Cam gave *herself* without reservation. That was his Cam.

Frank loved her in his own way. He had loved her almost her entire life. He'd loved her almost longer than his own life. Trapped in a light fixture that might have been a reject from the *Brady Bunch* set, he'd watched over her since she was four.

The house was too quiet. He knew too well the deafening roar of silence. For twenty years, Cam's voice had become the only sound he welcomed in the darkness of his world. She was light and life. The sound of her voice was almost enough to make him feel alive again.

Almost. It was only when he tried to touch her that he remembered he was dead.

He sat alert and attentive, ever vigilant. The tears Frank heard in Cam's voice made his throat ache. He knew every creak, groan, and sigh of the old house. The emptiness resonating through the house confirmed what he already sensed. Jim Stafford was gone, and soon Cam would be too. And he'd be alone again.

****

Grass roots ripped when the realtor pounded the For Sale *sign into the lawn. I felt like my guts were being torn out. The locks tumbled time after time, but the voices echoing through the empty rooms were never the one I wanted to hear. My mother was gone, and she left me there to rot.*

A chipper real estate agent's high heels clip-clopped on the hard wood floors. I eavesdropped on the whispered conversations as prospective buyers traipsed through his house. A woman mur-

mured, "It's perfect. I'll wallpaper in here. This can be Camellia's room." The anger and frustration that clogged my throat made me wish I could choke her.

I wanted to scream at her. Tell her to get out and never come back. I wished I knew how to make any of the hundreds of eerie ghostly sounds Hollywood used to instill fear in potential home owners. I wracked my brain trying to figure out a way to make the toilet bilge with black sludge like in The Amityville Horror, or pull a Ghostbusters and slime them when they poked their heads into closets.

The too-perky realtor extolled the virtues of the neighborhood, bubbling like a fountain as she gushed about the superiority of the school district. The man spoke only in a low rumble, his voice a deep, quiet hum too low to make out. When the front door closed behind them, I knew they'd be back.

The screech of a light bulb being screwed into a socket grated on my nerves.

"See, Cammie? It's perfect." Satisfaction sang in the woman's voice. "Now we have a light to read by."

She turned the switch. The light bulb sprang to life, and a jolt of electricity shot through me. The next thing I know, I'm flying across the room like some cartoon coyote shot from a cannon.

"Whoa!" I stumbled into the wall, breaking my momentum with my hands.

The woman smiled, settling on the bed next to a little girl, a book clutched in her hand.

"Now, where were we?" she asked as she opened to the page marked with a yarn-tasseled bookmark. "Ah, yes. Here we go."

I blinked to clear the spots from my eyes. A golden glow flooded the room. The walls, which had once been blue, gleamed bright white. I had to blink three more times before the intricate pattern of tiny rosebuds on the wallpaper swam into focus.

I turned and stared at the duo snuggled on the narrow twin bed. The woman's sleek, dark hair shone in the lamplight. The little girl stared at me solemnly over the top of the book, her blue *eyes wide and curious. I scowled at her, but instead of screaming, she clamped her pink lips together.*

I froze, plastering myself against the wall while the woman continued reading aloud. I tuned in to the words. I recognized the storyline. I almost swallowed my tongue when she said 'Jacob Marley'.

"Scrooge?" I asked, incredulous. "You're readin' Dickens to her? She's only a little kid."

The little girl looked up at me, but the woman continued reading as if I hadn't spoken.

"Is she some kind of genius, or are you trying to scare the bejesus out of your brat?"

I pushed away from the wall and crossed to the little girl's side of the bed.

"Next she's gonna tell you there's no such thing as ghosts. Well, take a good look, kid. You're starin' at one."

The girl only blinked, her blue eyes wide but untroubled.

Her unflinching stare freaked the Dickens out of me. "You see me?"

Just then, her mother whispered, "Sleepy?"

Cam nodded, answering them both at the same time.

Her mother turned her head and pressed a loud, smacking kiss to the little girl's temple. "I love you, my precious flower." She closed the book and rose. "Goodnight, my miracle," she whispered, reaching for the light switch.

A strange sucking sensation tugged at me the minute she touched that switch. A low primal groan of pain seeped from my lips. The little girl jumped.

"No, Mommy."

The woman smiled. "You want me to leave the light on until you fall asleep?"

Cam nodded and turned onto her side, her eyes wide open and fixed on me as she burrowed into her pillow. Her mother kissed her one last time then tiptoed from the room.

I stared straight into her bright blue eyes and drew myself to my full height. "You're not afraid of me?"

She shook her head, her golden-brown curls swishing against the pillowcase.

That irked me. I took a step closer to the bed. "Why not? Didn't you hear me? I'm a ghost."

Cam simply shrugged, her pink rosebud mouth pursed.

I held up my hands like claws. "Boo!"

The girl didn't jump or cry for her mommy. I turned to look at my hand, but I barely recognized it. It wasn't callused from tinkering with tools. My knuckles weren't embedded with grease and oil. They were smooth, hairless, childlike little hands.

Panic surged through me. I looked down at the faded Metallica shirt. It hung in loose folds from my shoulders. The faded 501s sagged from too-narrow hips, threatening to drop at any time. I made a grab for the waistband, hauling the denim up.

"What the hell?" *My hair flopped over my forehead. It hadn't done that for years, but I pushed it back with an impatient flick.*

"What's your name?" *she whispered.*

"Frank," *I answered automatically.*

"How come you're a ghost?"

I shook my head to clear it and hiked the jeans up with both hands. "'Cause I'm dead, kid."

"How come you're dead?"

"I got shot."

"Who shooted you?"

Resentment bubbled in my throat. I gave her my fiercest glare. The urge to tell the little brat everything that happened to me in minute, horrifying detail threatened to break free. The words rose in my throat, clawing their way up until they burned my tongue, tart and bitter. I opened my mouth to let them escape, but she peered up at me with those guileless blue eyes.

I kept my trap shut and shook my head. Twisting the denim in one fist, I vaulted over the bed. Suddenly I wanted to feel that pull. I needed to escape. I needed to think. I reached for the wall sconce. The cool, ridged metal of the switch felt good against my skin.

"How old are you?" the little girl lisped.

I glanced from her to the miniature version of my own body drowning in oversized clothes. I had absolutely no idea how to answer that question. My fingers closed around the notched spindle at the base of the lamp and I did the only thing I could think to do.

"Get the hell out of my room," I hissed and turned out the light.

****

To this day, Frank would swear the soul-sucking pain that crushed him when the light went out was almost orgasmic compared to the swirling morass of confusion that usually plagued him after an encounter with Cam.

This night would be no different.

Cam shifted and stirred, jolting him from his thoughts. When he looked at her, she met his gaze as directly as she had so long ago.

"I've missed you, Frank."

When he didn't answer, Cam rolled to the edge of the bed and reached for her foot. Tugging at the spiked heel of her boot, she pulled her foot free. "How've you been?"

The casual tone of her question made him laugh. She'd always been able to make him laugh, even when he wanted to cry from frustration.

"Dead," he answered succinctly. "And you?"

"Oh, I'm still alive," she muttered. She yanked the pointy-toed boot from her other foot and let it fall to the floor. "So, you missed me, huh?"

The shallow dimple in her cheek winked at him. He knew each of her smiles well enough to know this one was the real deal, not one of the fake smiles she'd practiced in the mirror above her dresser a decade before. He didn't respond. He didn't dare to let himself.

"Good," she said, swinging her legs over the edge of the bed. "I hope it sucked for you."

"Isn't Purgatory supposed to suck?"

"Is that what we're calling it now?"

"Nothin' better."

She gestured to the hideous seventies-era light fixture screwed into the wall, and said, "My mother called it a sconce."

Frank glared at the cone-shaped lamp which had become his prison. "Maybe I should call it Hell now that you're back."

She smiled, but this smile was different. This smile nearly bought him a one-way ticket to the fiery pits. Cam had a smile that made you ache to bask in the pure, feminine pleasure radiating from her.

"Don't do that," he grumbled, edging his way toward the wall.

"Gonna run away again?"

"I didn't run away." He ran his hand over the bristling strip of hair clinging to his scalp. "I'm dead, Cam. Dead," he reiterated through clenched teeth.

"Funny, you never seem dead to me." She stared at him for a moment. "When you ran away, I pretended you really were."

"I'm not pretending. I. Am. Dead."

Cam stood, closing the distance between them in two strides. She pressed her hand to his cheek, cupping her palm. He leaned into her touch, closing his eyes so he could ignore the thin strip of blue-white light separating her skin from his.

"You don't feel dead," she whispered.

A sob of frustration tangled in his chest, eddying in a never-ending whirlpool where his heart used to beat.

"I kissed you. I kissed you, and you kissed me back. Nothing dead could ever taste so good," she murmured.

He pressed into her hand, instinctively seeking the warmth of her caress. He wanted to experience the tickle of her breath against his lips. His throat was rough and ragged, torn to shreds by the longing welling inside of him.

"I can never be what you want me to be," he rasped. "Why can't you understand that, Cam? I can never *be*. Not anymore."

"I want you..."

"No!" He jerked back, wrenching himself from the lure of her touch.

"I need—"

"So much more than I can give you," he finished in a rush. He reached for the light switch.

"I'll turn it back on," she threatened.

"I won't come back."

"But you'll be here. You're always here, Frank. I can feel you here."

His fingers twitched against the grooved spindle on the sconce, caressing every worn ridge as they rasped against the whorls of his fingerprint. Her heartbeat pulsed in the room. Each breath she took rushed straight for the black hole in his chest, but nothing could fill the void.

He had the ability to touch everything, but when it came to Cam, all of his senses failed him—including common sense.

"But I can't feel *you*, Cam. Welcome to my Hell," he whispered and turned off the light.

Chapter Two

Cam didn't follow through on her threat to turn the switch. The pearly gray light of dusk seeped through the blinds. Pinpricks of rain spattered the window, keeping time with the staccato beat of her heart. She stood still, the air vibrating around her.

Questions. She had so many questions for him, but she knew she wouldn't get answers. Frank didn't answer questions, nor did he ask them. He preferred to lecture or chastise.

Frustration bubbled inside of her, roiling through the blood rushing in her veins. She reached for the blinds, threading her fingers through the slats until they pressed against the cool glass. She flattened her palm against the pane, fighting back the rush of pain threatening to engulf her.

"I can't believe he's gone," she whispered. "My Dad, not you. I'm not trying to lay a guilt trip on you. I just...I have no one."

Tears threatened again, but this time she let them fall. A watery laugh edged with hysteria erupted from her lips. "Maybe I am trying to guilt you. You're all I have left."

She closed her eyes when the electricity humming through the room kicked up a notch. He was listening. Whether he wanted to or not. Frank listened to every word she said, even if he lacked the balls to face her.

"I was going to say, I want you to stay with me." Sliding her hand through the slats, she balled her fingers into her fist and lowered it to her side. "I was trying to tell you I just need you here."

She turned on the light and held her breath as she waited for him to appear. When he didn't, she exhaled in a rush. "Okay, fine. That's not all I was trying to say, but it's true," she confessed.

Cam dropped to the edge of the bed, a tiny smile quirking her lips when the mattress bounced under her. "Ass," she hissed to the empty room. "Stubborn ass."

She spread her hands, palms turned up in supplication. "If I promise not to molest you, will you come back?"

The energy buzzing through the room ebbed. He retreated further and further away, leaving her alone.

"Damn it, Frank!"

A tingle of awareness flared and then faded once again. "I was a virgin," she blurted, "when you kissed me. A twenty-one-year-old virgin. I was waiting for you."

Another power surge sent shivers down her spine. "Does knowing that make you feel good?"

Cam rolled back on the bed, her socks sliding over the worn cotton comforter as she stretched like a cat. She raised her arms over her head and closed her eyes.

"I wanted you. I wanted your hands on me. You taste like spearmint and beer. You smell like Polo and motor oil. Something else too. Metal, I think."

"Blood."

Cam's smile widened as she opened her eyes. Frank stood beside the bed, his body haloed by the glow of the lamp. "Blood," she exhaled.

"Don't do this, Cam. We used to be friends."

"We can still be friends," she promised, reaching for his hand.

She laced her fingers through his, marveling at the shimmering silver light radiating from his skin.

"I remember when you came back after the first time. The night my mom died." She pressed the back of his hand to her cheek. "You said you didn't want to be friends."

He laughed—a short, sharp bark of derision. "I was right. Should've stuck to my guns."

"But you came back. You kept coming back." Cam brushed her lips to his knuckles. "We grew up together."

"No, you grew up. I'd already grown up. And died," he added, trying to extract his hand from her grip.

"You were my best friend. I told you everything."

Abruptly, she released his hand and swung her legs over the side of the bed. Frank stared at her, his eyes widening when her knees bracketed his legs.

"You wanted me," she whispered.

A sardonic smile twisted his lips. "A guy would have to be dead...Oh wait, I am."

Cam met his gaze. "I went back to school and fucked Ryan Miller the next day."

Frank flinched and turned away. His Adam's apple bobbed as he swallowed her words.

"Then I fucked one of his roommates the next weekend."

"Stop."

"I couldn't stop. I wouldn't stop, Frank. No one made me want like you do."

He reached for the light switch, and Cam batted his hand away.

Her fingers gripped his, and she stood. "Why are you such a coward?"

"Back off," he growled.

She shook her head and pressed her hand against his chest. "When I'm not here, I can almost convince myself you don't exist—"

"I don't."

"That I don't know you, you don't know me," she continued, ignoring his protests. "But you do. You were here. Every day. Every night. Watching me. Waiting for me."

Cam released a shuddering breath. Her hands slid across his chest, the peeling print on his tee shirt tickling her palms. Her fingers curled into the taut muscle of his neck, and the fight drained from her body.

She melted into him, burrowing into the soft cotton to hide her face. His arms encircled her—warm, solid, and safe.

"Frank."

"Don't do this."

His voice cracked on the plea, and she smiled. "I can't help it."

"I hate those guys."

Her smile widened, but she kept her face hidden. "I figured you would."

"We can't do this," he whispered, burying his face in her hair.

"I understand."

"Do you?"

"Yes." The word came out in a sigh. She pulled back, her hands gripping his shoulders as she lifted her gaze to his. "What am I going to do?"

"You've gotta go," he said in a rush. "Your dad is gone. You've nothing left here, Cam. Sell the house. Don't look back."

"I can't."

"You need to."

"What about you?"

"I'm dead. What happens to me doesn't matter."

Cam's hands glided over his shoulders until she cradled the back of his shaved head. She stroked the thin strip of his Mohawk. "No."

He fixed her with a ferocious scowl. "Now who's the stubborn ass?"

"I love you."

His hands closed around her wrists like iron manacles. He jerked her hands from his head, grasping them tightly between them while he stepped back. Heat shimmered between them. The light from his skin glowed white as lightning against hers in the dimly lit room.

His voice rumbled low and rough. "You have no idea who or what I am."

Cam stared back at him, tipping her chin at a belligerent angle. "You were shot. A drug deal gone wrong," she recited, unable to mask the tremor in her voice. "You died in the ambulance on the way to St. Sebastian's."

He blinked in shock but didn't refute her research. Frank released her wrists and stepped back. His boot caught the edge of the throw rug, and he stumbled into her dresser, rocking the bottles of long-evaporated perfume clustered on a mirrored tray.

"They caught the guy a few months later. Ballistics matched, and he pled out—turned over on some other guy and was sentenced to twenty-five years with possible parole," she continued.

"You're not... How did you...."

"I'm a writer. I can do research," she answered, crossing her arms over her chest. "You wanna hear what else I found?"

"No."

"Your mother remarried. You said she went to work for an insurance agent after your dad was killed, right? Wait, you didn't tell me. Mrs. Kelly did. You never told me anything," she accused.

"It's none of your damn business."

"You made it my business the night you popped into my room."

"I don't have a choice!"

"You do too." Cam took a step closer to him. "You choose when you show up. You choose to stay away."

His forehead creased, the frown bisecting his dark brows. "Cam." He sighed dejectedly.

She pounced. "I want to be your friend." When his wary gaze met hers, she laughed. "Okay, I want to be more, but I'll take friend if that's all I can get. You never told me anything, Frank. You never answered any questions. What was I supposed to do?"

"Why do you care what happened?"

"I care. I *need* to know. And maybe...if I do, I can let you go," she said cautiously.

He gave her a dubious smirk. "You think?"

"The questions just keep nagging me."

"And if I tell you things, if I answer your questions, you'll go? You'll sell this place and move on with your life?"

"If that's what you want. But you have to tell me the truth," she added, pinning him with a pointed stare.

Frank sighed and ran his hand over his Mohawk. He stepped around her, and he perched in his customary spot on the edge of the bed. His hands dangled loose and limp between his knees. He stared at her, his dark eyes wary like a trapped animal.

"What do you want to know?"

Cam blurted the first question that came to mind. "Do you love me too?"

Chapter Three

Bradley Mitchum turned the steering wheel with the heel of his right hand. His left propped his pounding head.

"Stupid, stupid, stupid," he muttered under his breath. His fingers dug into his temple, attempting to stem the flow of blood pulsing in his ears.

The trip to D.C. was supposed to be a quick in and out. As the newly appointed Creative Director of Honeycutt and Fitzgibbons Advertising, he and the managing partner of their firm plotted and planned their strategy for weeks. They were scheduled to fly out Sunday night, woo the client Monday afternoon, wine and dine him in the evening, and head back to the hotel for a good night's sleep before their six a.m. flight. Things had not gone according to plan.

They had no way of knowing the CEO of Inteli-Corp was a booze hound who hated to drink alone. They weren't aware that trailing the man and his merry band of sycophants from bar to bar was required of anyone who dared to court his business. Brad hadn't anticipated the rush of hot humiliation which flooded his veins when a man more than twice his age called him a pussy for attempting to beg off.

As he turned onto his street, Brad kept his breaths soft and shallow, trying to cause his body as little disturbance as humanly possible and calm his mind at the same time. He had to watch his step. A Creative Director coming up from the art department was unusual—a fact the ad men under him liked to point out in a number of not-so-subtle ways. He hoped Terry Fitzgibbons was more impressed with his pitch than IntelliCorp's CEO had seemed.

His gaze scanned the street, noting the drying puddles of rainwater along the curbs and the pale green leaves reaching for the spring sunlight. His shoulders dropped, and he lowered his hand. The knot of tension inside of him eased.

This would always be home. He grew up on this street—in the house that was now his. When his parents announced their plan to retire to Arizona two years before, Brad jumped at the chance to buy the house. His sisters thought he was nuts, but he didn't care. He wanted to live there. It was the only place he'd ever felt at home.

He wasn't a city guy. Brad only moved into an overpriced downtown apartment to avoid any possibility of becoming the creepy thirty-year-old guy who still lived with his parents. He moved out the second he closed on the house. He liked having a lawn to mow. He didn't mind cleaning gutters. Truth be told, he kind of liked having nosy neighbors.

The engine of his BMW purred its approval as he shot across the last intersection. He spotted Mrs. Kelly puttering in her yard and smiled.

"Speaking of nosy neighbors," he muttered under his breath.

Then he spotted a battered white Chevy Cavalier parked in Jim Stafford's drive. His foot slipped from the gas. Somehow he went from detached suburbanite to full-fledged nosy neighbor in zero to sixty flat.

Camellia never visits during the week. Hell, she hardly visits at all.

The Beemer drifted toward the curb, and he had to jerk the wheel and swing in a wide arc to make it into his drive. He hadn't even killed the engine before Mrs. Kelly crossed to the low fence separating their properties.

He yanked his briefcase and suit bag from the back seat and called, "Hi, Mrs. Kelly."

"Oh, Bradley, I'm so glad you're home," she said as he crossed the lawn. "Jim Stafford passed yesterday."

Brad froze, the strap of his bag sliding from his shoulder. "He did?"

"Yes. Massive coronary. He just fell out of his chair at the office."

"That's horrible." Brad's gaze drifted to the dented car in the Stafford's drive.

"Camellia is home. Poor thing, she's there all alone." She sighed. "I offered her Veronica's old room, but she said she had too many calls to make."

Brad stifled the smile that threatened the moment Mrs. Kelly mentioned her daughter's room. The doll collection she harbored for her only daughter was the stuff of legends. Tales of Veronica Kelly's dolls seeking blood-soaked revenge was once a playground favorite in their town.

He found Mrs. Kelly staring at him expectantly. "Oh. Yeah. Uh, that's rough." He scrubbed his face with his hand. "Has she made any arrangements yet?"

"I think they were working on them today. She seemed a little shell-shocked yesterday. I took her a tuna noodle casserole."

This time the smile won out. "I'm sure a hot meal helped," he told her, hoping he sounded sincere.

She stared pointedly at his bag. "Have you been traveling, dear?"

"A quick trip. I'm taking the rest of the day off, then back to the office tomorrow." He cocked his head. "Looks like we got some rain."

"Oh, it was a miserable day yesterday."

"It sure was," he muttered under his breath. He squinted into the bright spring sunlight. "I'm gonna pull the lawn mower out and clean things up a bit."

Mrs. Kelly stepped back from the fence, her gaze darting toward the house. "Bradley, would you mind..." she trailed off, waving vaguely to the grass on her side of the fence. "Bob's knees aren't good."

He had to smile. Bob Kelly's knees were fine. The old guy just preferred to exercise his wrist by pointing the remote at the television. He'd been cutting the Kelly's lawn and Jim Stafford's since he moved back to Warrenton, but each spring he and Mrs. Kelly did the same little dance.

"No problem. I'm happy to help."

She smiled. "You're a good boy, Bradley. I'll bake oatmeal cookies for you."

"Thanks." He backed away from the fence. "I'm gonna go for a quick run. Maybe things will dry out by the time I get back."

Once inside, he dumped the suit bag in the foyer, toed off his shoes, and began unbuttoning his shirt. The wrinkled blue button-down pooled on the floor where it fell. His thin white undershirt followed, then his belt. By the time he reached his bedroom door, the weight of his wallet and keys dragged his pants to his ankles, and he stepped out of them.

Clad only in black socks and gray boxer briefs, he tumbled forward onto his bed, planting his nose in the comforter. He inhaled deeply and mustered the strength to roll to his back, blinking at the ceiling.

"Camellia." He sighed.

Covering his throbbing eyes with his forearm, he conjured an image of Camellia Stafford—the girl almost-next-door. The conjuring didn't take much effort.

He'd watched her for years. She'd always been pretty, even when she went through the horrible awkward phase most teenage girls seem to go through. By the time she started her freshman year at Warrenton High, he was a senior and she was a knockout. Most people never bothered to notice. Cam's beauty was a quiet kind of beauty, and her figure a tad too Rubenesque for fashion's fickle tastes, but Brad Mitchum would have loved to taste her.

He closed his eyes and pictured her as he saw her two summers before. She'd crawled out of her decrepit old car, her wavy caramel-colored tresses whipping into her eyes. Dainty hands captured the wayward strands while she sashayed up the walk, pulling them back to reveal smooth, creamy skin. She bent to sniff a stargazer lily. He never could erase the memory of the pleasure-soaked smile lighting her face when she straightened.

Then she caught him staring...at her ass.

What an ass she had. Round and high, filling the backside of her cargo shorts to mouth-watering perfection. Brad's scotch-sodden body stirred at the thought.

Cam quirked an eyebrow at him, waggled those graceful fingers, and laughed as she pushed through the front door to her father's house.

Brad groaned, remembering the deep flush that flooded his cheeks when he realized he'd been holding the garden hose at crotch level the entire time he'd ogled her.

The heat crept into his cheeks again. He rolled up, gripping the edge of the mattress to minimize the sloshing in his stomach.

"No self-flagellation today, pal—at least, not *that* kind."

Pushing off of the bed, he staggered to the dresser and yanked open a drawer. He changed into running clothes, muttering under his breath, "Just sweat it out."

Two minutes later, he let himself out the back door. In the shadow of the house, he paused to stretch. His head throbbed, blood rushing in his ears as he bent at the waist, clutching his knees.

"Suck it up," he muttered.

Giving his torso a few twists for good measure, he started down the drive at a brisk walk and picked up to a sedate jog by the time he hit the sidewalk.

He tried to convince himself that turning toward the Stafford's house was habit rather than design. He usually turned in their direction for morning runs, reversing his course on the days when he got his two miles in during evening hours. His feet were entitled to a little confusion. He didn't often jog at noon.

He wanted to believe mere curiosity drew his gaze to the white car parked behind Jim's rain-spotted Buick. He'd heard enough bragging from her proud father to think Cam could afford a more reputable vehicle, but she chose to hang onto the heap for some reason.

Brad snorted softly and shook his head. An admitted car snob, he couldn't conjure any valid excuse for driving such a car.

He fixed his gaze blocks ahead, focusing on his first goal. He'd need two miles at a minimum to sweat the scotch from his system. Once he took care of his hangover, he'd figure out how to uncover more about the elusive Camellia Stafford.

Chapter Four

Yes.

The word reverberated in her head, slipping its way into every thought since she'd opened her eyes. They'd talked until the sunrise shimmered on the horizon, and then she'd slept. Cozy and safe, she'd burrowed into him. The light was out, and Frank was gone when she woke, but she knew he would be.

Bright sunlight streamed through the blinds, laddering the worn hardwood floor and capturing dust motes in its rays. Cam rubbed the sleep from her eyes and reached for the drawer of the nightstand. She needed to write the answers he'd given her down before they drifted away. Frank always drifted away from her in the light of day.

Yes.

'Yes' was the only word that mattered. Even if everything else faded into the misty wisps of a dream, she would never forget he said yes. Scribbling furiously, she did her best to recall every question she'd asked and every answer he'd given. She clutched the ancient spiral-bound notebook she left in the drawer for this purpose. She'd learned her lesson long ago. If she wrote it down, he was real, and she needed him to be real.

Her cell chirped, jerking her back to reality. Cam lunged for the nightstand again.

"Crap," she muttered. She noted the time and leapt from the bed, stumbling toward the hall. "Crap, crap, crap."

****

No!

The word caromed around in his head, bouncing off his skull with nowhere to go. He would have shouted out loud, but the effort wouldn't matter. No one would hear.

Frank heard everything: the rustle of the bedclothes when she rolled over that morning, the scrape of the nightstand drawer, the crinkle of paper, and the soft whoosh of ink flowing onto the page. He knew exactly what she was doing.

She was turning what should be harmless dreams into memories.

Frustration boiled inside of him. He wanted to snatch the pen from her fingers. He itched to tear the pages from her notebook. He ached for the caress of the puffs of breath that escaped her lips as she wrote. His resistance was futile. She was going to write every answer down, and he couldn't do a damn thing to stop her.

He didn't think much about the diary when he first spotted the little book. How could something with a cartoon kitten on the cover be a threat to someone facing the specter of eternity? This torment started not long after Cam's tenth birthday. Some brilliant little brat had given her a diary. Two books were filled and shoved to the back of the nightstand drawer before he discovered what she was doing.

At thirteen, Cam was chock full of idiotic romantic notions. That's why she was writing everything down like some kind of permanent record. Every conversation they'd ever had. Every tidbit of knowledge he'd inadvertently let slip. She believed the click of the flimsy gold lock kept her secrets safe, but he knew neither of them was safe. If she wrote their secrets out, that made everything they were to each other too important, and everything they would never be all too real.

They'd fought. They always fought—like cats and dogs or brother and sister—but this fight was different. He'd never forget the fingers of dread balling into a fist in his gut when she told him what she wrote in her diaries.

****

Cam sat straight on the bed. I perched in my usual spot on the edge of the mattress. Her hair was a wild tangle of riotous curls, the result of the permanent she'd talked her father into letting her have. Pink tinged her cheeks, but her innate determination shone in the blue gaze fixed intently on me.

It was like being run over by a truck.

"What?"

"You want me to repeat it?" she retorted.

The panic swelling inside of me must have shown on my face because Cam pounced, ready and willing to exploit any sign of weakness. "No!"

"I want you to be the one."

"You're nuts," I sneered.

"I'm serious. Chrissie Rand said Brian Hoyt kissed her last night. He was her first kiss." She tipped her chin up, leveling him with her direct gaze. "I think it's time I had my first kiss, and I want you to kiss me."

I ran my hand through my too-long hair and sprang from the bed. "You're only a kid."

"You're not that much older than me!"

I whirled and glared at her. "I'm twenty-three, Cam."

She rolled her eyes. "You don't look twenty-three."

"Because you're only seeing me the way you want to see me!" Something told me it was safer to keep moving, so I began to pace the room. Then, I grasped it. The argument to end this ridiculous argument. "Actually, I'm thirty-four." I smiled, waiting for the truth to take root in Cam's fertile mind.

"You definitely don't look thirty-four."

"I was born in 1963. You do the math if you don't believe me."

Cam swung her feet from the bed and glared at me. "It's just a kiss," she argued.

"And I'm just dead!" I shook my head and held up both hands to hold her off. "This isn't real, Cam. This is all a dream. You're going to grow up, some other guy will kiss you, and you won't even remember this."

"Yes, I will."

"No, you won't."

"Bet me," she sneered.

I clenched my jaw until it ached. No one could do stubborn like Cam. "This isn't real. You and me, we're just a dream or something."

Cam jerked the nightstand drawer open and pulled out two locked diaries. "It's not a dream! I wrote it all down!"

"You what?"

"I wrote it all down. Everything," she announced in a defiant tone.

I stared at the books. I swear, I could hear the ticking of a bomb. She held tangible evidence of my existence—or lack of existence—in her hands.

"You shouldn't have done that." I didn't know the reason why, but judging by the grasping pain around the hole in my heart, I knew I spoke the truth.

"Well, I did, and you can't read them. They're locked."

I reached for one of the journals, but it slipped through my fingers like smoke. The nerve endings in my fingers burned. I jerked my hand back and cupped it in my palm. My mind raced. My fingers tingled. Desperation gnawed at my gut as I searched for a different tactic.

I extended my hand palm up and whispered, "Cam, please."

She shook her head, pressing the books to her chest. "No. They're mine—my private thoughts and feelings. You can't have them."

"But...you can't write that stuff." I carefully kept my voice calm and cool.

She quirked a challenging eyebrow. I knew it was a faint foreshadowing of the woman she would become. "Yes, I can, and I did."

"Give them to me."

"Give me a kiss, and maybe I will," she replied coolly.

"No."

"Then I have to say 'no' too."

Bristling, I straightened my spine and threw my shoulders back, matching her defiant glare. "I'll go, and I'll never come back."

Cam flinched, and I instantly regretted the words.

"You wouldn't be the first one," she said quietly. "Get out."

"Cam—"

"Go. Either kiss me, or get out of my room," she said, tucking her chin to her chest to avoid my gaze.

The tremor in her voice didn't mask the steel that lay beneath her words. I pressed my lips together and gave serious consideration to both options. Silence echoed through the room. A full minute passed before she raised her head. That's when I saw the flash of hope in those vibrant blue eyes.

The hope hit me harder than a punch in the gut. Without a moment of hesitation, I reached for the switch on the lamp. "Goodbye, Cam."

****

He'd stayed away after she told him about the diary. At first it was hard. She left the light on every night, but he didn't dare show himself. Wrapping his fingers in the electrical wires, he held on tight, resisting the pull of her. He closed his mind, refusing to listen to her whispered pleas. He thanked God his heart no longer beat, for he was sure it would have leapt from his chest when she cried into her pillow.

He stayed away for a month, then two. She stopped crying herself to sleep. By the time it turned into six, she stopped pleading with him. When the days melted into month twelve, she started turning out the light before she fell asleep. The first year was the hardest. The second seemed easier for her, if not for him.

She still talked to him. Somehow she knew he was still there. Shortly before her sixteenth birthday, she told him that some punk named Mark Howard manned up and kissed her. Certain Cam's adolescent ardor would be directed toward someone more appropriate—someone more alive—Frank determined it was safe enough to venture into her life again. For the next five years, their friendship resumed without missing a beat.

Trapped between one world and another, he kept his promise, listening to her as she talked of her hopes and dreams, arguing her choices with her as she debated one college versus another, and standing helplessly by as she packed her clothes and stereo and moved into a dorm room a hundred miles away.

Frank absorbed the loneliness pulsing through Jim Stafford's veins when he stepped into the empty house each night. He became acutely attuned to the tone of the older man's distracted humming, learning to anticipate Cam's imminent arrival by faint strains of an old Simon and Garfunkel song, *Homeward Bound.*

Frank knew he was weak. Cam always made him weak. When she curled up on the bed the night before, tears drying on her cheeks, he had to comfort her. It was all he was good for. The tracks of her tears coiled around him, constricting his soul. The apology he whispered was meant to cover a myriad of sins.

She smiled at him, and the choke-hold of those tears eased. She smiled at him, her eyes lighting with enough love and trust to make his soul ache.

****

Cam was thirty minutes late for her one o'clock appointment with the Funeral Director. The slippery dry cleaning bag tucked under her arm tried to make a break for it when she slammed the front door. She slid behind the wheel and jammed the key into the ignition. The bag holding the suit, shirt, and polka-dotted tie she'd chosen for her father slithered to the floorboard. She retrieved it and draped the bag over the passenger seat.

Yes.

She chose to ignore the terse, 'Not that it matters,' Frank added to his admission and shot out of the drive in reverse. Instead, she focused on the one word she wanted to hear. He'd said 'yes' so clearly and distinctly she almost didn't believe her ears.

She zipped through town, deep in thought. Stoplights lost all meaning. The red octagonal signs on the corners? Purely decorative. Nothing meant anything to her except the 'Yes' that meant everything.

Frank loved her.

She hissed between her teeth as she turned into the empty parking lot of the funeral home. She parked under the portico along the side of the building and grabbed the dry cleaning bag from the seat.

Cam climbed from the car and glanced at the gleaming white columns standing sentry at the front door. Her father's body lay inside, but deep in her heart she knew he was already long gone. He was with her mother, his Lily.

She straightened her shoulders and marched up the steps, grateful to have these last minutes alone with the one person who knew what it meant to love a ghost.

****

Cam winced at the squeak of her brakes when she parked behind her father's Buick once again.

"Gotta get that done," she muttered under her breath.

The buzz of a weed whacker filled the air. She climbed from the car and extracted some hanging clothes and a suitcase from the back seat. The suitcase bumped behind her as she hurried for the front door, the plastic hangers dangling from the clothes draped over her arm clattering with each step she took.

Inside the cool, dim house she hung the suit and dresses she carried in the hall closet and abandoned the suitcase near the door. She made a beeline for the kitchen, only to stop in her tracks when she spotted the remnants of the previous day's kitchen catastrophe hardening on the floor. She wrinkled her nose and covered her mouth with her hand, stepping over the mess to open the back door and let the fresh air into the room.

"Ick, ick, *ick!*"

Cam unspooled half a roll of paper towels and covered the congealed casserole in a strawberry printed shroud. She blessed her father's memory as she located the commercial-sized jug of spray cleanser he kept beneath the sink and gingerly lifted the towels to spritz the grayish gunk stuck to the linoleum.

"Stupid..."

Cam set the bottle aside and straightened, reaching for the handle on the refrigerator door. She inspected its contents while the cleanser permeated the putrid pile, opting for a bottle of beer over the out-of-date orange juice in the door.

She ran the pad of her thumb over the dimpled edges of the cap and took a long pull from the bottle. Moving to the screen door, Cam noticed that the grass in the backyard was already too long. The flowered heads of spring weeds poked through the scraggly blades. She picked at the label on the bottle with her thumbnail, rolling the cap against the palm of her free hand. The motor of the weed whacker cut out, and suddenly the demanding chirps of nesting birds took over.

She glanced at her neighbor's yard expecting to find Mr. Kelly storing his lawn implements in the detached garage. Instead, Cam sputtered, choking on a swallow of beer as she admired the gleaming golden-brown skin of a nicely muscled back. She thumped the heel of her hand against her chest.

"Good for you, Mrs. K," she murmured admiringly.

The man bent, disappearing from view below the fence-line.

"Oh, no! Don't go, you pretty, pretty thing," she breathed, moving closer to the door for a better view. When he straightened again, she smiled. "Much better."

The smile slipped a notch when the man turned toward the fence. She took a hasty step back to avoid being detected and cocked her head to keep him in sight, drinking in the details.

A thin line of toffee-colored hair rose from the waistband of a pair of blessedly low-slung cargo shorts. Her smile returned full force as she saw his long fingers curl around a belt loop and hike the shorts higher.

"Too late," she whispered into her beer bottle.

The smooth hair on his stomach gave way to a dusting of wiry curls on his chest. They shone with the sweat glistening at his throat, trickling over the long, sleek muscles lining his shoulders. His biceps bunched when he hoisted the grass trimmer over the fence, depositing it in the too-tall grass of her yard.

Cam took another step back, her brow puckering in confusion as the latch on the gate between the Kelly's property and hers gave way with a loud chink. Moments later, a bright green lawn mower rolled through the gate propelled by its luscious lawn jockey.

He closed the gate with what appeared to be a practiced flick of his wrist and bent to unscrew the gas cap on the mower.

As soon as she could gather her wits, Cam punched the lever on the screen door, sending it sailing wide open. "Excuse me!"

The door slammed against the house, capturing his attention. His head jerked up, and his eyes widened when he spotted her.

Undeterred, Cam took a step forward. Pretty creature or not, the guy didn't belong in her yard. "Excuse me, what are you doing?"

The man straightened then glanced around the yard as if the answer should be obvious. "Well, I was gonna mow," he began, a sardonic smile lifting one corner of his mouth. "Why? You got a better idea?"

"Yes." Cam shook her head, regretting the word the minute it slipped from her lips.

Yes.

She closed her eyes, blocking out the echo of Frank's voice. Opening her eyes again, Cam fought to keep her voice even while she pinned him with a glare.

"Why do you think you're going to mow my yard?" she asked stiffly.

Planting his hands on his hips, he scanned the yard again. "I always mow your dad's yard, Camellia," he answered, his voice deep and fathomless.

Cam reared back, trying to place the voice. There was something familiar about his face. "You do?"

"Well, for the past couple of years," he amended.

"You have?"

"No. I just made that up so I'd be free to roam around people's yards showing off my equipment." Cam's lips quirked at his choice of words, and he held up one hand to stop her. "Mower. Weed Eater. Lawn care equipment," he clarified with a mischievous smile.

"Uh huh." She smiled and leaned against the rail of the back steps. "You must be the guy who bought the Mitchum's house."

His smile morphed into a grin. "Yeah, I'm the guy." He moved closer to the steps, wiping his hands ineffectually on his grass-covered shorts. "And you are Camellia Stafford."

"Cam," she corrected, extending her hand.

His fingers closed around hers. A thousand volts of electricity jolted her body. She blinked, staring into his earnest green eyes. "You're Bradley," she murmured. A puzzled frown creased her brow, and her voice grew tentative. "Bradley Mitchum?"

"Brad," he answered, a warm smile lighting his features.

"Whoa. Bradley Mitchum. You bought your parents' house?" she asked, incredulous.

He laughed, the deep rumble of it vibrating low in her stomach as she carefully extricated her hand from his. "I'm not sure if I should be more insulted by the sneer I hear in your voice or the fact you didn't recognize me. We grew up two houses apart."

"And a few years," she added, instantly defensive.

He tossed her a rueful smile and shrugged sheepishly. "I'd have known you anywhere, Camellia."

Feeling oddly short of breath, she whispered, "Cam."

"Cam," he repeated low and soft.

"Brad." She took a deep breath and forced a smile. "You do look a lot different. You used to be all tall and gangly."

His eyebrows rose. "You mean I shrank?"

Warmed by his playful tone, she gave him a deliberate once over. "Well, you aren't gangly anymore."

"Thanks for noticing."

He approached slowly, and for a split second Cam wondered if *Animal Planet* was secretly filming in her backyard. He was sleek and stealthy, his footsteps cushioned by the tall grass, his emerald eyes fixed on her like she was his prey. The sun lit a faint white scar running vertically under the copper-brown curls on his chest, and she itched to run her finger along its path.

He bent his knee, resting one foot on the bottom step and returned the favor, those cat's eyes taking in every detail as they swept upwards. When they came to light on her face, she had to blink back the urge to confirm she was still dressed.

"I'm sorry about your dad," he said, his voice deep and soft. "I liked him a lot."

Taken aback by the swift change in subject, Cam had to shift her brain into overdrive to catch up. "Thanks. He...uh, he must have liked you, too. I mean, he didn't let just anyone mess with his lawn."

Brad chuckled softly, and Cam's gaze dropped to his chest. Her mouth watered as she eyed the glimmering beads of sweat clinging to the hollow of his throat. "I had to audition using Mrs. Kelly's lawn, of course," he explained, gesturing toward the fence.

"Of course."

He leaned in, pressing his weight onto his bent knee. "I'll tell you a little secret I discovered."

"Oh?"

"Your dad hated yard work."

It was Cam's turn to laugh. "You'll never make it as a spy."

"I'm serious. The flowers, yes," he conceded, nodding toward the front of the house, "but not the yard."

Her mind raced, a thousand little details about her dad filtering through her brain. She sifted through them, looking for a clue, any clue, to substantiate Brad's claim. Cam realized she could come up with about a dozen clues too easily. She stared at him for a moment then frowned as she looked past his shoulder at one of the overgrown camellia bushes.

"You might be right," she murmured.

Brad pulled back, hiking his shorts up again and resting his hands on his hips. "I guess I should get to it. I thought I'd clean things up. I figure you'll have family around this week—"

"It's just me," Cam answered without thinking. When his face darkened with concern, she shook her head and tried to smile. "I do have an uncle. Barney," she quickly added. "He was my mom's brother. Is, I mean. He's still alive—lives in Wichita, of all places." She cringed, and a nervous laugh escaped her.

"Wichita, huh?"

"He won't be coming. He's probably about eighty now, and he and Daddy..." She trailed off, wishing she'd wadded the paper towels she'd left on the kitchen floor into her mouth instead. "It'll be a small service," she stated flatly.

"Visitation?"

Cam nodded. "Tomorrow evening. No funeral, though. Just a graveside thing."

"I see."

"He had it all planned out." Her voice snagged, and she clamped her mouth shut tight. Turning back toward the house, Cam blinked back a hot rush of tears.

"He liked a good plan," Brad said, his voice smooth and gentle. "I used to get a kick out of the garden diagrams."

A laugh bubbled around the sob caught in her chest. "On graph paper, no less."

"A four square cube equaled twelve inches of bed space."

"Every bulb recorded in detail." Cam smiled at the glistening golden god staring at her, puzzled by the blunt admiration shining in his eyes. Running a self-conscious hand over her hair, she asked, "Do you want a beer?"

"More than my next breath," he replied, favoring her with a brilliant smile. "Will you keep it cold for me? Until I'm done mowing?"

She edged to the door, having a hard time dragging her gaze from him. "Will do."

"I'll be there, by the way," he called after her.

Cam froze, her fingers curling around the handle of the screen door. She turned back to him and spotted the color rising high on his cheekbones.

"Tomorrow, I mean. I'm sure a lot of people will...but just so you know, I'll be there too."

Cam stared at him for a second, arrested by his firm, quiet statement. "You will?"

"Yes."

She tensed, struck by the power of a single word spoken clearly and distinctly. Inclining her head, she gave him a tremulous smile and dashed into the house.

Cam took three steadying breaths, glaring at the paper towels strewn on the floor and trying to figure out exactly how a simple acknowledgment of intent could leave her completely shaken.

****

The screen door slammed. Frank heard a lawn mower sputter to life. He squeezed his eyes shut, concentrating on Cam's every movement. He tried to will her into the room, silently begging her to turn on the light. They needed to talk about those damn books.

Frank passed the day trying to figure out what to do about Cam's notebook. He also needed to get those little locked journals stashed at the back of the drawer. He knew he had to do something, anything, to make them disappear. It galled him that she was still writing about him, and there still wasn't a damn thing he could do to stop her.

How is it possible that I can touch everything in this room, including Cam, but I can't get a grip on those damn books?

Cam bustled around the kitchen, muttering and cussing under her breath. The house vibrated with her agitation. She scraped something against the floor murmuring 'Sorry, Charlie' under her breath.

Water ran in the sink. A bottle of liquid soap belched loudly. The clank of dishes piled in the drainer set his teeth on edge. The quiet hiss of spray cleanser whispered in his ears, and a squeak of cleanliness marked the end of her task.

"Ugh," she groaned.

A plastic trash liner slithered as it was pulled from the can. The hinges on the screen door creaked, the bag of trash hit the back porch with a soft splat, and the door slammed against its frame.

"Come on. Come on," he muttered.

She shuffled through the living room, straightening picture frames and ashtrays that were never used. A stack of newspapers and magazines fell into the recycling bin with a thunk. A pillow was plumped by several vicious blows.

Her heels pounded the floorboards as she hurried to the bathroom. Frank gritted his teeth while drawers opened and closed. The door of the medicine cabinet banged against the wall.

Cam hissed in frustration and hurried back to the front door. Plastic wheels rumbled along the varnished floors; something softer bumped against the frame of the bedroom door.

"That's right, beat yourself black and blue, you idiot," Cam murmured.

She grunted and heaved something onto the bed, and the box springs protested the abuse. "Come on, Cam, turn on the light," Frank prodded.

Cam gathered some clinking bottles and cans and hurried back toward the bathroom. She hummed tunelessly, nearly drowning out the sound of caps popping open and compacts snapping closed. The thwap of a curling iron's tongs echoed down the hall. The sound of the lawn mower drew closer to the house.

Frank scowled at the intrusion. Focusing harder, he picked up the thread of the old Simon and Garfunkel tune when she strolled back into the room.

"I wish I was..." she sang under her breath.

Fabric rustled and her voice was muffled. Cotton scraped over skin. She rummaged through the suitcase again, shaking something out with a sharp snap. Her shoulder popped as she pulled on a shirt. The teeth of a zipper meshed.

She hummed the next few lines of the song, and Frank stilled, an arrow of fear embedding itself in the void in his chest.

The buzz of the lawn mower receded. Frank wondered if Cam thought he was the one who was supposed to wait silently for her. He resented the implication. He wasn't waiting for her, he was stuck here.

Her footsteps padded down the hall. Static crackled from the stereo. The refrigerator opened and closed. A bottle cap plinked against the counter. Another cap followed, and Frank frowned in confusion.

The screen door opened and closed, and the lawn mower cut out abruptly.

"Ready for your beer?" she called.

Then it struck him. Someone else was waiting for her.

The ragged edges of the gaping wound in his chest prickled. The rumble of another man's voice hummed in the air, and Frank could only whisper, "No."

Chapter Five

The mower droned. The vibration masked the trembling of Brad's fingers. The jolts sang joyfully up his palms, wrists, and arms. He focused solely on the patch of grass in his path. The severed blades spewed from the mulcher, leaving trails of destruction in his wake. He turned the corner at the front of the lawn and glanced up.

He moved on autopilot, watching as a minivan rolled out of the drive across the street and headed in the opposite direction. A garden hose lay coiled in the neighbor's yard, its nozzle attached to a daisy-shaped sprinkler.

The memory of a bright yellow Slip 'n Slide stretched over the same lawn flashed into his head. Julie Edwin's father had set the strip of plastic up for her. Within minutes of attaching the hose, the neighborhood kids had found their way into the yard. Except for him.

He sat on the front porch with a sketch pad in his lap, trying to ignore the shrieks of delight carrying on the summer wind. At twelve, he was a little older than those kids and he wanted to think he was too cool to fling himself bodily onto a strip of water-soaked plastic. Intent on his drawing, he wanted to believe he was happy where he was—safe and dry, tucked in the corner of the porch swing with a giant box of colored pencils.

Green. The pencil he had been holding was a dark green. He'd been using it to color the forest of trees he'd sketched into the panel. He snapped it in half as he stared at the laughing, squealing kids lining up again across the street. He remembered glancing at the smooth, flat sketch pad in his hand. He recalled his fervent wish that he wasn't too old and too cool to take the plunge. He remembered Cam standing in line for her turn—her pudgy, baby-soft arms crossed over her bathing suit.

Brad stared straight at Jim Stafford's house and his jaw tightened. He promised himself this time he wouldn't be too cool. This was his turn. He wasn't the kid sitting safe and sound in the shadows of the porch anymore.

His fingers brushed absently over the sliver of a scar at the center of his chest. He drew a deep, determined breath and pushed the mower a little harder. Sweat trickled from his temple to his jaw, running into the crevice of his ear to elude the swipe of his hand. Anxious to claim his prize, he covered the front lawn in record time. He forged his way into the back yard and the towering camellia bushes caught his eye.

He'd asked Jim about them one day. His offer to trim them back was met with a sad shake of the older man's head. "I like them wild and free," was all he said.

Turning the mower, his head jerked up when the screen door slammed.

Cam's hair hung in tousled waves around her face. The breeze picked at a few strands, tossing them willy-nilly. Wild and free.

She smiled at him, holding a bottle of beer aloft. "Ready for your beer?"

He stopped and stared, taking in the worn, faded jeans molding to her curves and the snug pink tee shirt that wavered somewhere between enticing and indecent. The lettering on the front stretched across her breasts. The script spelled 'Dream', and for a moment he wondered if he was in one.

The mower buzzed in place, scalping the young blades of grass and giving lie to the manufacturer's claims of self-propulsion. He switched it off and tugged his damp shirt from the handle.

"More than ready," he answered, high-stepping through the grass to make his way to her.

"You look hot."

He smirked, opting for his own interpretation of her statement. Condensation filmed the cool glass, but her fingers were warm to the touch. He accepted the bottle and raised it in a toast.

"Thanks. So do you."

Cam laughed and tossed her mane of hair over one shoulder. "Wanna come in?" she asked, reaching for the handle on the screen door.

Brad grimaced at his grass-spattered shins and shoes. He dragged his arm across his forehead and wrinkled his nose. "I'm pretty ripe," he demurred, lifting the bottle to his lips again.

Cam gave him a saucy smile, nodding to his sweat-sheened chest. "And juicy."

He choked on his beer, shaking his head and turning away to thump on his chest.

She stared at him, her eyes wide and innocent. "Oh, I'm sorry. Can you only dish it?"

He shook his head again and swallowed hard. "No. I can take it."

Cam smiled as she started down the steps, scooting past him toward the side of the house. "Come on, we'll sit on the front porch in the shade."

He followed her, fascinated by the clumps of grass stuck to the soles of her feet, and mesmerized by the sway of her hips.

Charcoal, he decided. *Not pastels or watercolors. Well, maybe oil pastels,* he conceded.

Cam climbed the first two steps and settled on the top. She squinted up at him and murmured, "You're tall."

He took the hint, lowering himself to the third stair from the top and turning toward her. "Better?"

"I didn't mind the view before."

"I liked it from where I was standing too." He planted his grass-stained shoes on the walk and leaned back, bracing his elbows on the step behind him.

"Were you this tall in high school?"

He nodded, eying the hastily cut lawn critically. "Since I was about sixteen, I guess."

"I don't remember you playing basketball. Shouldn't someone so tall play basketball?"

He smiled at the tiny furrow of confusion creasing her forehead. "I'm only six-four—not tall for a basketball player."

"So you did play," she concluded.

"Nope."

"Why not?"

He worried the edge of the label with his thumbnail. "Never had any talent for basketball."

Cam laughed. "Our team always sucked. You'd think they'd be grateful for the height."

He sat up, leaning forward to brace his arms on his knees. "I'm not good with games. I didn't play many sports when I was a kid."

"Why not? You've got the build."

"But not the stamina," he added with a wry smile. "Then. I didn't have the stamina, *then*. I promise, my stamina is fine now," he stated firmly.

Her laugh was husky, like whiskey laced with honey. "Is it?"

Drawn to her laugh like a fly, he turned to look her straight in the eye. "Yes."

She grinned and saluted him with her beer. "Good to know."

He switched gears, angling for a more neutral topic. "Your dad told me you're a writer, like your mom. Are you penning the great American novel?"

Cam shifted and her gaze drifted to the flowerbeds. "Well, first, I use a computer to write, so there's no pen involved. Second, unlike my mother, I don't write fiction. So, no," she concluded quietly.

"Non-fiction? Self-help? Hey, did you write the manual for my DVR? 'Cause that thing was a bitch to hook up." It was a desperate attempt to garner another laugh and chase away the clouds dulling her vivid blue eyes.

A tiny dimple flashed when she turned back to him with a smile. "Mainly magazine articles, but I have tackled a couple of technical writing assignments. They're boring, but they pay decently."

"And you travel?"

"Sometimes."

"Your dad said you were going to Mexico."

The clouds came back, and he wanted to kick himself—hard.

"I did," she answered flatly.

They lapsed into silence, lifting their bottles in unison. A cricket chirped in the shade of the hedges. He searched his brain for something to say that wouldn't remind her of her parents. Somewhere down the block, a child shrieked with laughter and he felt his heart clench.

"What do you do?"

"Your car looks like it's gonna collapse from exhaustion in the drive," he said at the same time.

"I'm the Creative Director for an ad agency, Honeycutt and Fitzgibbons."

"My car is fine," she said, talking over his answer.

Brad chuckled and shook his head. "Your car is a wreck."

They lapsed into silence once more, and the vise gripping his heart squeezed tighter.

"You won some art contest in school."

"You never write fiction?" he blurted.

Cam gave a breathless laugh. "We're going to have to start taking numbers."

"You go first," he prompted.

"Art contest?" she repeated, raising an inquiring eyebrow.

"Scholarship," he corrected.

"That's right. I remember they had a painting or something in the front lobby. Black and white, like a maze."

"Charcoal. Part of my Escher phase."

"Oh. Just a phase?" she asked, a teasing light brightening her blue eyes.

"Post Picasso, pre-nudes," he confirmed with a nod.

"Nudes, huh?"

He grinned at her speculative tone. "I had to wait to go to college for the nudes. My mom wouldn't have appreciated the purely aesthetic qualities of some of the models."

"I bet."

The cricket chirped again, serenading them with a screeching song. When she didn't answer, he opted to withdraw his question. He drained his beer and placed the bottle on the top step. "I should finish up. It'll be dark soon."

"I never thought I'd be any good," she admitted quietly. "You know, sharing the stuff going on in my head, dreaming things up and making people believe them."

He sat still, waiting for her to elaborate. Another cricket chimed in, making it a duet. "Did you ever try?" he asked softly.

Cam favored him with a small, sad smile. "That was my mom's thing. I'd spot an ant carrying a crumb, and the next thing you know she's created an entire underground civilization thriving in my backyard."

"*Antillium.*"

Cam jerked, her eyes flashing with surprise. Awe and annoyance edged her voice as she cocked her head and asked, "You know that?"

He gave her a reluctant nod. "A crumb to one is a feast to many," he quoted, his gaze locked on hers. "Your mom gave my mom copies of her books. The short stories. I loved them."

A dreamy smile curved her lips. "I did too."

Brad jumped in—hurtling himself bodily down the slippery slope. "What are you doing for dinner tonight?"

Cam blinked, rearing back at the sudden change in topic. "Are you asking me out?"

"No. Well, yes, but not right now," he rambled. "I mean, yes, I'm asking you out, but for another night. Tonight, I was wondering if you wanted to come over for pizza. I have something I want to show you."

Her inquisitive eyebrow rose again. "Your etchings?"

He smiled, delighted by the genuine interest in her vivid blue eyes. "Something like that. Will you?"

Cam raised one shoulder then nodded. "Sure, why not? I'm fresh out of tuna noodle casserole."

He laughed and leaned closer to her. "Shh. Don't say that too loud," he whispered. Scooping his wadded tee shirt from the bottom step, he waved toward the back of the house. "Give me an hour or so. I'll finish the lawn and run home to shower."

"Don't run!" she called after him. "I wouldn't want you to break a sweat or something."

He laughed, heading for the backyard to reclaim his mower. "Definitely don't want to sweat *that* out," he muttered under his breath.

****

Exactly one hour later, he was freshly showered and dressed in jeans faded enough to be casual, but lacking the paint and varnish stains his more well-loved pairs sported. He'd just pulled the cork from a bottle of merlot when the doorbell rang.

"Please tell me you have high-speed Internet," Cam said, clutching a laptop to her chest as she sagged dramatically against the doorframe. "Cable, DSL—anything but dial up."

Brad couldn't help but grin. He ushered her in with a sweeping gesture. "I'm even wireless, ma'am."

Cam beamed at him, giving his long-sleeved thermal shirt and jeans an appraising sweep. "I didn't think I saw any pesky cords."

"Right this way."

"You are a knight in shining armor."

He led her toward the kitchen. "Ah, but the password may cost you," he teased.

"Whoa! Wow," she exclaimed, coming to a dead stop in the living room. Turning in a slow circle, she gave the open space which served as living room, dining room, and kitchen an admiring inspection. "The house wasn't always like this, was it?"

"Nope." He gestured to the granite-covered breakfast bar dividing the dining area from the kitchen. "I gutted the place when I closed. Still working on the guest bath, and I haven't made it to the other bedrooms yet."

"This is incredible," she enthused. Placing her laptop on the counter, she ran her fingertips over the brushed nickel drawer pulls. "Do you hire out?"

He chuckled, pouring a generous amount of wine into a paper-thin goblet. "Once I'm done with this I'm never hammering a nail again."

"It's amazing, Bradley. Brad," she amended, taking the glass of wine he offered her.

She clutched the bowl of the glass to her chest, eyes glowing with pleasure as she reached to touch the tawny shade of a pendant light suspended over the bar. His body tightened as she continued her tactile tour of the kitchen—stroking the stainless steel cooktop and caressing the maple trim of one glass-fronted cabinet.

"I'm glad you like it," he said gruffly. When she glanced over at him, he cleared his throat and pointed to the laptop. "Is it an emergency?"

"I just need to check my email. I was hoping to land an assignment and they were supposed to let me know either way."

He popped the latch on the cover and tipped it open. "The password is 'MadMan1980'."

She grinned, placing her glass next to the computer. "I love that show."

"Yes, the glamorous world of advertising is really like that," he drawled before taking a sip of his wine.

The laptop whirred to life. "Good. I was worried you weren't getting enough scotch and sex in your diet," she quipped.

He winced, recalling the crippling hangover he suffered that morning. "Don't say scotch. I'm never drinking scotch again."

She glanced up, her azure eyes dancing with amusement. "What about the sex? You swearing off sex too?" she asked sweetly.

"Nope. Still all for the sex," he retorted, meeting her gaze directly. Inordinately pleased by the faint blush rising in her cheeks, he pushed away from the counter. "I ordered the pizza. I hope you eat meat."

"Now *that* was a nice segue," she commented, tapping on the touchpad to open the Internet connection.

He snorted. "I'm not so smooth."

He was smooth enough, however, to press his hand into the small of her back when he peered at the screen, setting his glass next to hers. "MadMan1980. Capital M's. Take your time. I'll be right back," he promised, scooting past her.

As he strode toward the back bedroom, he heard her call out, "Can I at least pick your brain on the home improvement stuff?"

He snatched a sketch pad from a cardboard box and fanned the pages. "Sure," he shouted back. He plucked another book from the box and started to flip through the sketches. "You have a yen to camp out at Home Depot?" He tossed those books aside and pulled two more from the box. "I have an impact wrench you can borrow."

Cam whooped, and he straightened. Brad snagged the rest of the pads from the box and carried them back to the kitchen. "Good news or was that for the wrench?" he asked, propping his shoulder against the refrigerator.

"A series."

"On what?"

She smirked. "Dating in your thirties and forties."

He barked a laugh. "What are you, twenty-five? Twenty-six?"

"They don't know how old I am."

"That has to be fraud," he murmured. Brad closed the book and set it on top of the fridge.

"It's a living," she muttered, exiting out of the email program. "Mama needs money for hammers and nails."

Distracted by his quest, he asked, "What do you want to remodel?"

"Well, I figure I'm going to have to do some work on the house in order to sell."

His head snapped up. "You're selling?"

Cam reached for her wine, her brow furrowing as her fingers wound around the stem. "Why would I hang onto it? It's too big for just me. I'd never be able to keep up with the maintenance."

He blinked, processing her words. "Yeah, I guess so," he muttered, looking at the page in front of him. A smile quirked his lips when he found the drawing of a gray mouse wielding a sword and shield.

He flipped back to the title page and held the sketch pad out to her. "My etchings."

Cam shot him a puzzled look and set her glass aside once more. She scanned the page then gave him a startled glance. "*Greystone Manor?*" she whispered.

"I loved comic books, wanted to draw them when I grew up. I loved your mom's stories too."

Cam blinked rapidly, her eyes searching his. Averting her gaze, she turned the page, shaking her head in disbelief. "You drew a comic book about *Greystone Manor?*"

He smiled, unable to resist tucking the lock of hair curtaining her cheek behind her ear. "I think the cool kids call them graphic novels now." She looked up, tears pooling in her eyes. "Please don't cry. I wanted to make you happy. You know, comics? Happy?" he cajoled.

Cam reached for him. Her soft hand closed around his, squeezing tightly. "I am happy," she whispered.

"Could've fooled me."

"I'm a woman, we cry when we're happy."

"Remind me to work on making you miserable."

Cam laughed, her hand slipping from his. He watched as she traced the outline of one of the panels reverently.

"You can have the book if you want."

"I want," she whispered.

"On one condition," he quickly added.

"Oh?"

"You never answered me. About the date," he reminded her.

She gave him a watery smile, knuckling away a tear that clung to her eyelashes. "I'm gonna be busy for a couple of days," she said, her voice soft and tremulous.

"I know." The doorbell chimed, and their heads swiveled toward the front of the house. "I'll be there tomorrow. I'll be here whenever you're ready," he said softly. "Just say yes."

Cam looked at him wide-eyed and whispered, "Yes."

He smiled. "I'll grab the pizza and you can tell me how you think I did with Lord Rodant Earsamore."

Chapter Six

Cam tiptoed through the front door like a teenager trying to elude detection, but Frank was on to her. The water ran in the bathroom sink. She hummed as she brushed her teeth. She spit, slurped some water, and spit again. The towel rack squeaked. She sang 'Homeward Bound', her voice muffled by terrycloth.

The yearning in her voice pummeled him, knocking him back in time. For years, he listened for her, waiting for her increasingly infrequent trips home. She never spoke to him. She didn't call his name. During those years he didn't need to fight against the pull of her because she wouldn't reach for him. Then, one night she did.

****

Cam switched on the light.

"Frank?" Her breath hitched and I tried to steel myself against her siren song. "Frank, please. I need to see you."

Cam's quiet desperation speared me in the gut. I closed my eyes and let go, giving in to the lure of her. I took form beside her bed. I'm pretty sure my jaw cracked when it hit the floor. I could feel my lips moving, but the only sound that came out was a strangled groan.

"Hello, Frank," she whispered, drawing one knee up in a provocative pose.

I couldn't help but look. I couldn't tear my eyes from her if my afterlife depended on it. Lush, ripe curves barely contained by a scrap of snowy white lace called to me. Her nipples pressed against the sheer fabric. The tight pink buds made my mouth water. The lingerie clung to her narrow waist and cut high over rounded hips.

Her skin stretched like cream velvet over firm, smooth thighs. Her toenails were polished a devilish red.

"What the hell?" I managed to croak at last.

"I've been thinking about this a lot," she began in a low, husky voice. "I want you, Frank. I want you to make love to me."

"No!"

She swung her shapely legs over the edge of the bed then rose in one graceful move. God, she was beautiful.

"I've thought about it a lot. It's all I think about. You're all I think about."

This couldn't be happening. It shouldn't be happening. I knew I had to stop it. I had to prove to her once and for all that this wasn't real—we weren't real. At least, I wasn't. Cam was all too real a threat as she took a step forward. I lunged for the nightstand drawer, making a desperate grab for her journal. My fingers wouldn't close around the pages. I wanted to howl with frustration.

She pressed her hand to my back, but no sensation crept through the cotton. "Frank, look at me," she whispered.

"No!" I tried to snatch the notebook from the drawer, and again it eluded my grasp.

"Look at me."

I straightened but kept my back to her. I was afraid. "I can't! Why are you doing this?" The ache in my voice made me cringe, but it was nothing compared to the tightening in my jeans.

"Frank."

I squeezed my eyes shut and slowly turned to face her. "What?" I snapped.

Cam wound her arms around my neck, her fingers grazing the strip of close-cropped hair that ran down the center of my skull. My head almost exploded. "You know what."

I tried for a sneer, but I probably missed by a mile. "Make love? What the hell have you been reading?"

Cam raised one eyebrow. "Fine, fuck me," she said in a taunting tone.

"What the hell do you think I am?"

"You're my friend. You've been here for me. You've been watching me, waiting for me. I've been waiting too. I'm not a kid anymore, Frank, I'm a woman. I'm a woman who wants you."

Okay, I admit it. I peeked at the lace-clad curves pressing against me. I watched her hands slide down my arms. I saw her fingers curl into my biceps. A small, appreciative moan gurgled from her throat. My body stirred, but the hell of it was I couldn't feel a thing. She moved closer, her full breasts flattening against my chest, her hips moving instinctively against mine.

"Kiss me," she whispered.

God help me, I did. I pressed my mouth to hers. I crushed her lips, bruising them in my quest to know if they were as plush as I imagined. Cam moaned again and my hips jerked. I cupped the rounded curve of her ass and angled my head, taking the kiss deeper when her lips parted in surprise.

Her tongue tangled with mine, but I couldn't taste her. Her flesh filled my hands, but I couldn't feel her. Her spun-gold hair spilled over her shoulders, but its scent remained a mystery to me.

I caught her moan with my mouth. I braced myself against the sheer force of her, planting my feet. She gasped when I pulled her closer, molding her body to mine.

Heat surged through me, the blood in my veins boiled—trapped in the immortal prison of a body long dead. I stumbled back, scraping the back of my hand across my mouth in a vain attempt to erase any trace of this entire debacle.

"No," I rasped, staring straight into her wide blue eyes.

"Yes."

"Never. It will never happen."

"Now. I want you now," she retorted, lifting her chin.

"No."

Her eyes glittered with the sheen of angry tears. For once, we were on the same wavelength.

"Yes," she whispered, moving closer again.

The longing in her voice nearly broke me to pieces. Frustrated and angry, I lashed out in the only way I knew how.

Grasping her shoulders, I pushed her away. Fear flashed in her eyes. My lip curled into a sneer. My voice came out cold and mocking— my father's voice dripping like venom from my lips. "Sorry, kid, I'm just not feelin' it," I growled. Then I plunged us both into darkness.

****

He'd lied. When he kissed her, he felt too much, and nothing at all. It was the nothingness that clawed at him, making his skin burn with frustration. He needed to experience her soft, soothing caress. His body's response to a touch so hopelessly out of reach baffled him. He was scared the searing white light that flared each time they made contact would turn the tattered remains of his soul to ash.

Frank clung to a thin thread of self-preservation, holding himself still when she shuffled into the room. He didn't dare think about the night before. She had no idea how close they'd come. When she'd wrapped her arms around him, her lips hovering near his, she held his soul in her hands. If she had kissed him, he would have handed it over and been damned.

The button on her jeans popped and she expelled a gusty breath when she drew the zipper down. Cam sang in whisper. The lyrics wrapped around him, squeezing him in a stranglehold of tender memories. He listened intently to the rustle of fabric, and a moment later, he recognized the soft plop of a bra hitting the floor.

She heaved the suitcase to the floor and jerked back the covers. The mattress groaned. Her joints popped as she stretched. She drew a deep breath and let the last words of the song drift away on the oxygen seeping from her lungs.

He waited, but she didn't turn on the light. The bed frame creaked when she rolled onto her side. Her hair whispered against the pillowcase. Soft, shallow breaths grew deep and even.

He waited for her to call his name, but when a name sighed from her lips it wasn't the one he expected.

"Who the hell is Brad?"

Chapter Seven

Cam scraped her thumbnail against the pad of her index finger. She was certain there would be a groove there by the time the visitation was over, but the habit distracted her. It kept her from staring at the stranger in the gleaming coffin beside her. Her father was gone, and with him the quiet surety that had cocooned her all of her life.

She leaned over, accepting the hug the diminutive Mrs. Hollings from the next block insisted she needed to give her. Her eyes strayed to the door, scanning the area where the guest book stood on its podium for any newcomers. There were none.

She listened with half an ear, nodding mutely as the tiny woman waxed poetic over the sprays of floral arrangements flanking the casket. Her gaze drifted to a potted Peace Lily with a tiny white card which read, 'With our deepest sympathies, The Mitchums'.

The visitation started twenty minutes before, with only a few elderly people—veterans of the funeral home circuit, no doubt—trickling in the moment the doors to the viewing room opened. She'd accepted the condolences of her father's neighbors and business associates as graciously as possible, but her thoughts were scattered.

Her inner turmoil centered on the news she'd received when she'd met with her father's attorney and Tom Haskell, his partner in the accounting firm the two men had founded more than thirty years before. She'd been flummoxed by the numbers they tossed around so casually.

Jim Stafford had left behind a sizable estate. Not enormous, but more than enough to keep her comfortable for many, many years, even if she never accepted another writing assignment.

When she'd returned to the house that afternoon, she'd tried to puzzle it out while answering the incessant call of the doorbell and ferrying casseroles and serving platters from the front door to the kitchen. Marjorie Crutcher, her father's long-time secretary, stood in the kitchen arranging and rearranging the refrigerator as each new offering threatened to overthrow the system.

Cam fidgeted with the pencil the older woman had been using to note the contents of each dish and the name of the person who had delivered the condolence.

"Mrs. Crutcher?"

"Sweetheart?" Marjorie moved a tray of pinwheels to the top shelf.

"My dad ... I met with Mr. Sheffland and Mr. Haskell today," she began tentatively.

"Mmhmm."

"I was just... I guess I need to figure it all out. This house, the life insurance... There's a lot of money."

Marjorie chuckled as she withdrew from the depths of the refrigerator. "Well, I'm not surprised. After all, your daddy spent his days messing with money."

"And his evenings messing in the flowerbeds," Cam murmured.

She turned, fixing Cam with a sharp glance before her face softened. "Yes. That was what he loved to do." She held her arms out in invitation, and enveloped Cam in a tight hug. "And he loved you. You were his life's work. Everything he did was for you, to keep you safe and secure."

Cam broke down, dissolving into the comfort of Marjorie's plump body, and clinging to the familiar scent of peppermint and Estee Lauder's Youth Dew. She sniffed and drew back, wiping her eyes with her fingers. "I'm gonna miss him so much."

Marjorie smoothed Cam's hair with the same motherly caress she'd employed for ages. "I know, Sweetheart. Me too." She drew a shaky breath, and gave Cam a watery smile. "Don't worry about the other stuff, Tom will help you," she said gently. "All you have to do now is go wash your pretty face and get dressed."

"Yeah," Cam acceded with a nod.

With a wave to the plates, platters, and pans covering almost every square inch of counter space, she said, "I've got everything under control."

With those reassuring words, Cam was able to get herself under control. Now she stood calm and collected, surrounded by gladioli and enveloped by the scent of carnations. White lilies and roses blanketed the casket. Simon and Garfunkel accompanied the never-ending loop of photographs displayed on a flat screen mounted in the corner.

She raised her head in time to catch a snapshot of her parents grinning proudly at the bundle of pink blankets nestled between them. Her father's dark blonde hair was neatly combed, but his striped tie was casually askew. Her mother's flowing mahogany waves cascaded over her shoulder, spilling onto the blanket and nearly shrouding the billowing white peasant blouse she wore.

Tiny hairs on the back of her neck prickled, and Cam turned toward the door. Mrs. Kelly approached, her hand tucked into the crook of her husband's arm. Veronica Kelly Distler followed, but Cam's gaze didn't linger on Veronica's bulging belly. She stared in shock at the tall man in the gray suit scrawling his name in the guest book.

"Camellia," Mrs. Kelly murmured, slipping her hand from Bob Kelly's arm to grasp Cam's.

"Thank you so much for coming," Cam responded automatically, trying to focus on the task at hand.

"We'll sure miss your dad, honey," Mr. Kelly said, giving Cam's shoulder a squeeze.

"I'm very sorry," Veronica chimed in over her mother's shoulder.

"Thank you."

Her gaze drifted toward the back of the room, but Brad had turned away. His broad shoulders almost filled the doorway. The tailored fit of his suit accentuated the long, lean lines of his body. A woman approached him, and he pulled her into a warm embrace.

"Thank you," she repeated, jerking her eyes from the couple in the doorway. She glanced down, and a nervous laugh erupted from her lips. "Wow. Look at you." She gestured to Veronica's burgeoning baby bump.

"Ugh. Don't look at me," Veronica answered, pushing her hair back from her glowing face.

"You look amazing," Cam assured her.

"I wish I felt amazing."

When Veronica launched into a laundry list of complaints about her pregnancy, Cam tuned out. Her attention strayed to the couple at the back. Brad's arm was settled comfortably around the woman's waist. Artfully streaked brown hair swung over the woman's shoulder when she tipped her head back and treated Brad to a brilliant smile. He chuckled and bent to whisper in his companion's ear.

"But at least I'm not puking my guts up every morning anymore," Veronica finished.

"Well, that's something," Cam murmured.

"We should..." Mrs. Kelly interrupted, nodding to the casket. "Please let us know if there's anything we can do, dear," she said, nudging her husband and daughter along.

"Thank you," Cam said again. She spared the coffin a quick glance as they moved past then turned to face the rest of the room.

Brad's arm was still wrapped around the woman's narrow waist. He paused every few steps, greeting neighbors and exchanging a few words. His hair, so dark with damp the day before, gleamed in the recessed lighting. Cam picked up a fiery hint of auburn in its depths.

The woman's simple wrap dress hugged her lithe figure, draping over her slender frame. Matchstick thin heels brought the top of her head to Brad's ear. Cam peered at her dress, and decided she resembled a sausage in casing by comparison.

The dark charcoal gray of his suit combined with the sober lines of his face gave him a slightly forbidding air. The easy smiles he'd showered on her the night before were gone. The loose limbed movement of his body was masked by yards of fine wool. The knot in his tie was cinched snug at his throat.

He lifted his head, and his grass-green gaze pinned her with laser precision. Cam bit her lip when a hint of a smile twitched his. He turned back to the woman, murmuring directly into her ear.

Cam steeled herself as they approached, wetting her afflicted lip before forcing a small smile. "Hi. You came," she said inanely.

Brad stopped in front of her and smiled, the warmth of it melting the solemn lines of his face. "I told you I'd be here," he said, stooping to pull her into a hug.

The woman at his side cleared her throat, but Cam sensed his reluctance as he pulled away.

"You probably don't remember me," the woman said, her voice low and smooth.

"Oh! Yeah, sorry. Cam, this is my sister, Stephanie," Brad said in a rush, stepping aside.

"Stephanie," Cam repeated. Her stomach un-clenched as she took Stephanie's proffered hand. "Nice to meet you."

Brad's sister smiled. "You were just a little girl the last time I saw you."

"She's old," Brad explained, earning a sharp jab in the ribs.

"Pipe down, Puny," she hissed. Stephanie smiled at Cam. "He was the runt of the litter."

A laugh tickled her throat as Cam peered up at Brad. "Not anymore."

"Once a pesky little brother, always a pesky little brother," Stephanie intoned, but her affectionate glance at Brad gave her away. "I'm so sorry about your dad. I remember when your parents moved in. I wanted to be just like your mom when I grew up," she added in a conspiratorial whisper.

Cam chuckled as she glanced from one to the other, picking out the similarities and differences. "Sure, who wouldn't?"

Brad grunted, and Cam avoided his pointed stare.

"Thank you for coming," she murmured, falling back on the comfort of routine. Gesturing to the potted plant she'd been staring at earlier, she said, "Your parents sent a Peace Lily."

"My mom likes to cover all the bases," Brad observed with a gusty laugh. "She sent Steph because she was afraid I'd get caught up at work and wouldn't make it on time."

"Yeah, well, we know you can't be trusted when you're doodling," Stephanie said with a wry smile.

"Doodling," he snorted. "I was working, and I left exactly on time. Traffic," he grumbled.

Amused by their squabbling, Cam turned to Stephanie and asked, "Is he easily distracted?"

"Only by pens, pencils, paper, crayons, cars, and other bright, shiny objects."

"So, most anything," Cam concluded.

"Pretty much."

With a pointed glance over his shoulder, Brad said, "We should move on."

Disappointment welled inside of her. Cam curled her fingers into her palm, her nails biting into the tender skin. "Thanks again for coming," she murmured, schooling her features into a polite smile.

When they walked away, she forced herself not to stare after them. Cam riveted her attention on the next person in line, shaking hands, accepting hugs, and responding to concerned inquiries by rote.

A flash of gray in her peripheral vision tugged at her, but she resisted. A laugh registering a few decibels too loud for the hushed room snared her attention. Brad sat in the back of the room, his arm draped over Stephanie's chair. His sister pressed her fingers to her lips to prevent any further disruption. He met Cam's stare and his devilish smile faded, but his gaze remained warm and steady on hers.

A few minutes later, Stephanie rose from her chair. She patted Brad's shoulder and scooted out of the row. Cam watched as her fingers lingered on her brother's suit jacket.

A tingle of awareness tickled her when Brad turned to seek her out. She smiled, and he returned it, his features relaxing as he sat back. He sprawled on the chair, his attention focused solely on her as he made himself comfortable.

Chapter Eight

Brad unbuttoned his suit coat and dropped onto the chair next to his sister. He draped his arm on the back of her seat, and leaned in to ask, "Do you always have to make me look like an idiot?"

"My job as your sister," Stephanie answered. "Laura and I take our work very seriously."

"Yeah, whatever." He dug one finger under the knot of his tie and gave the silk a little tug. "You just totally made me look like a schmuck in front of the girl I'm gonna marry," he said in a grave tone.

Stephanie laughed and he couldn't help but grin when everyone turned to stare. He glanced up to find Cam watching them, and his triumphant smile lost all power under the confusion in her gaze. He stared back at her, trying to reassure her.

"I wasn't aware you were seeing anyone," Steph said in a low voice.

"I'm not dating her. Not yet."

"Oh, so you've just sketched this all out in your head," she concluded, giving him a conciliatory pat on the knee.

"I'll make it happen."

Stephanie gave a dubious chuckle. "By the sheer force of your will?"

"Worked for me for about thirty years now," he said, turning to meet her eyes.

"Be careful," she whispered, closing her hand over his knee and giving him an imploring squeeze.

"I gave up being careful a while ago."

"I can't help it, I have to say that. Force of habit."

"Get over it," he murmured, softening his words with a smile.

She gave him a wan smile in return and patted his leg again. "I should go. Rob and the kids are probably pounding the table with their knives and forks."

"Thanks for coming, Sis, but you didn't need to," he said as she rose.

Stephanie squeezed his shoulder, and shuffled out of the row. "Bye, Doodles," she whispered.

Brad sat back in the chair, watching as Cam greeted mourner after mourner, and wondering how she could hold herself together. She was all that was left of her family.

As much as his two older sisters loved to torment him, they loved to love him even more. Stephanie had been eight when he was born; Laura, ten. From the moment his parents brought him home, he belonged to them. Through thick and thin they'd always been on his side. They comforted him when he needed someone to understand, taunted him when they'd decided he'd been coddled enough, and ran interference for him when he needed a little breathing room.

Cam stood alone; calm, quiet, and heartbreakingly beautiful. Before he realized what he was doing, Brad rose from the chair and started toward the front of the room. By the time he reached her, he'd managed to close his jacket, but couldn't make himself stop fidgeting with the button.

"Can I bring you anything? Water? A cup of coffee?" he asked, eager to be of some use.

"Water would be great," she sighed, favoring him with a tired smile.

He abandoned the button, his fingers closing around the curve of her elbow. "I'll be right back," he promised, giving her arm a gentle squeeze.

****

Four hours later, Brad wound his way into Jim Stafford's kitchen. A quick glance confirmed she wasn't a part of the bustle. The door stood open. The cool night breeze wafted into the overstuffed house, but the gentle stir proved no match for the press of bodies inside.

He'd long since ditched his suit coat and tie. The cuffs of his shirt had been turned back twice and then ruthlessly shoved over his elbows. His thin cotton undershirt was damp against his back.

Brad snaked his way through the churning kitchen, smiling at the ladies refilling platters and plates, and grimacing at the stack of carefully labeled casserole dishes piled precariously in the sink.

A plump woman with a wedge haircut was clearly in charge, pulling tray after tray from the refrigerator and issuing instructions. She paused when she spotted Brad. A Jell-O mold loaded with miniature marshmallows quivered in the pie pan she held. She eyed him appraisingly, her gaze lighting on the bottles of beer caught between his fingers.

"She's outside," she said, jerking her head toward the screen door.

"Thanks."

The hinges protested as he opened the door, and he groaned his relief when the cool breeze wrapped itself around him.

"Good, huh?" Cam asked, peering at him from her perch on the top step.

"Like a sauna in there." He walked down two steps, and lowered himself next to her. "Here, I thought you could use this."

Cam smiled and nodded to the two unopened beers at her feet. "I figured you'd escape their clutches sooner or later."

A grin split his face. "Good. We won't have to go back in for a while."

She cast a wary glance at the screen door. "I've never seen so many people in my house."

"Your dad was well liked."

"Yeah, I guess it was hard not to like him."

"True."

A faint smile played at her lips. "They didn't like my mom so much."

"No? How do you know?"

"Oh, I'd hear them talking after she died. People forget kids have ears."

"True." He smoothed his thumb over the edge of the label on his bottle. "I'm sorry, Cam."

"She was different from them," she murmured, staring out at the darkened yard. "I've never met two people who were less alike than my mom and dad."

He stiffened at her rueful little laugh. "Must have worked for them."

"Yeah, it did. She was wild and happy and free, and he...wasn't."

"He kept her grounded. That's not necessarily a bad thing."

"No," she conceded in a whisper.

She blinked back tears. He watched her dark lashes flutter like a butterfly from brow to cheekbone. He switched his beer to the other hand and pressed his palm to the center of her back in a desperate attempt to keep her from taking flight.

The heat of her skin seeped through the thin fabric of her dress. She leaned back, resting a little of her weight in his hand.

"I own half a strip mall now," Cam blurted.

"You do?" When she nodded, he let his hand glide up her spine. His fingers curled around her shoulder, kneading the taut muscle. "A good one?"

Cam tipped her head forward, accepting his awkward ministrations. "Got a SuperCuts, a sub shop, and a liquor store."

"Ah, a money maker for sure," he chuckled. Brad set his beer aside and spread his knees wide. "Come here."

She glanced at him then at the space he'd made between his legs. "Wow. Still resorting to the old massage ploy?"

"A ploy that works," he answered, lifting his hand from her neck.

With a tiny grunt she stood and stepped daintily over his foot. She sat on the second step and braced her arms on his legs.

"Relax," he murmured, pressing his thumbs to the base of her neck.

She surrendered, falling back into the cradle of his thighs and heaving a slumberous sigh. "You're right, it does work."

He worked his knuckles along the sides of her neck, and she rewarded him with a low purr. Brad laughed, his fingers invading the smooth knot of her hair. "Can I take this out?" he asked, tapping the plastic clip holding the tawny waves captive.

"Please," she whispered.

Her hair spilled over his hands as the clip clattered to the steps. He cleared the lump from his throat and began to massage her scalp. His voice came slow and thick anyway. "So, you're a real estate mogul?"

"Mmhmm." Her hands slid over his knees in a caress that was anything but innocent. "I'm quite the catch now. You might wanna make a move."

His fingers froze. "I thought I did."

She craned her neck and shot him a coy glance. "Oh, you did?"

A sharp stab of anger speared his chest. "Are you playing with me?"

Cam blinked in surprise and started to pull away. He caught her, his hands closing around her shoulders, the squared tips of his fingers pressing into her skin.

"I'm sorry. I'm sorry," he said in a rush. His tone gentled. "I... Listen, flirt with me, tease me, but don't pretend you don't know I want you."

"Okay," she whispered, shooting him a confused frown.

"I'm sorry," he said again, releasing his hold on her.

She shook her head. "No, I get you." She turned to look him in the eye. "No games. You don't play games."

"I'm not good at them."

Cam nodded and settled back between his legs again. "Well, if we're being blunt, I want you to go back to what you were doing."

He smiled and slid his hands under the curtain of her hair, echoing her sigh when his fingers threaded through the thick mass. "God, you have beautiful hair," he whispered.

"I used to hate my hair."

"I spent all day mixing colors in my head. I'm still not sure I could get the shades right."

"Mixing colors?"

His thumbs pressed into the nape of her neck, and she tipped her face up with a groan. "Paint."

"You want to paint me?"

He laughed softly. "Not my strong suit. I do better with pencils or pastels, but I think you would demand oil paints."

"I would?"

"Vivid, strong. God, I'd need a Bob Ross-sized palette to have room enough to mix them all."

"Who's Bob Ross?"

"Never mind." His hands slid to her shoulders and he began to knead gently. "Can it be this weekend?"

"What? Painting?"

"You promised me a date."

She let her head fall forward and moaned her approval. "Shouldn't this count?" she asked breathlessly.

"No. This is comfort."

"You wouldn't say that if you knew what was going on inside me," she countered.

He sucked in a sharp breath then the air exploded from his lungs. "I wouldn't?"

"I want you to kiss me."

"God, I want to."

Cam straightened, her knees bumping his calf when she turned to him. "Then do it."

He bit his lip and shook his head slowly.

"You won't kiss me?" she asked, affronted.

"Oh, I will," he promised. "But not tonight. Or tomorrow," he hastily added.

"When?" she challenged.

"Any other day, you pick."

"Why not today or tomorrow? Why not right now?"

He frowned, staring at her indignant face. "Because your dad just died," he began in a bewildered tone. "Because you're sad and confused," he added, picking up steam. "I don't want to kiss you to make you feel better. I don't want you to kiss me because you want comfort or consolation or whatever."

"You think I'm that pathetic?" she sneered, scrambling from between his knees.

He met her glare with a defiant stare of his own. Brad pressed one hand to the worn boards and leveraged himself off the stair. "I think it's been a long, hard day. I think you're grieving."

"Well, aren't you chivalrous, Lord Earsamore," she spat, shielding her eyes from the glare of the porch light.

He saw the glitter of unshed tears as she tilted her chin as if preparing for a blow. He leaned down and brushed a soft, chaste kiss to her cheek.

His voice was low and taut, almost trembling against the tight rein he held on the impatience swirling inside of him. "No, I'm not chivalrous. I'm just selfish... Just selfish enough that I don't want to be the guy you kissed the night before you buried the first man you ever loved."

She stared at him, her eyes wide and her lips parted in confusion. He gave her hand a gentle squeeze. "Goodnight, Cam. Try to get some sleep," he whispered, and then he was gone.

Chapter Nine

Silence, blessed silence.

The cacophony of voices filling the house nearly drove Frank out of his mind, which was pretty inconvenient, considering he had no place else to go. He tried to hold it together. He searched and searched, but couldn't separate the one voice he wanted from the rest of the maddening crowd. He tried to block them all out, he screamed for them to leave. Of course, no one listened, no one heard.

The noise continued unabated for hours. With mind-splintering sluggishness, the crowd eventually dispersed, leaving behind only the hum of soft-spoken voices and the clamor of dishes being washed, stacked, and dried. The screen door opened and closed, and at last Cam's voice broke through.

"No, I'll help," she said. "I hid out all night. I just…I couldn't deal."

Another woman spoke. Frank didn't recognize the voice, but he fervently agreed with the sentiment when she shooed Cam away, urging her to go to bed, telling her she needed her rest.

The bathroom sink ran. Water splashed, Cam's fingers slapped against her face. The faucet in the kitchen shut off and the click of high heels bounced off the walls.

"I'll see you in the morning, Sweetheart," the woman said.

"Goodnight, Marjorie. Thank you," Cam answered.

Her voice sounded raspy and tear-roughened. A swish of fabric told tales of a prolonged embrace. A moment later, the heels beat a hasty tattoo on the hardwood floor, the front door closed, and the house was at last silent—blessedly silent.

Cam's footsteps whispered into the room. The floorboards creaked as she shifted from foot to foot, and the mattress whined in protest when she dropped onto the bed. She sighed, a drawn-out 'Ahh' that spoke volumes. The soft whoosh of fabric falling to the floor confirmed she had stripped off her nylons.

The bed squeaked again when she stood. Her dress and bra followed the nylons. Cotton rasped as she pulled clothes from the open suitcase on the floor.

She muttered under her breath when she crawled into the narrow twin bed. One harsh puff of air followed another. She fiddled with the comforter. A quiet tick, tick, tick rang through the room. Frank smiled. She was fidgeting.

Finally, she huffed, and turned the switch on the wall sconce.

"Get the hell in here," she ordered.

A laugh sputtered from his lips, but he stubbornly stayed put.

"Come here, or I'll go grab a screwdriver and disconnect this damn thing right now," she threatened.

Instead of being angered or annoyed by her imperious command, Frank was intrigued. He appeared at her bedside in the blink of an eye.

"Do you think that would work?" he asked without preamble.

"Hello, Frank," she replied in an arch tone.

He touched the base of the sconce, his fingers curving around the edges. "I can't believe I never thought of unscrewing the damn thing."

"Well, you're here, so I'm not unscrewing it."

He scowled, shooting her a dark look. "Not your choice."

Cam drew her knees to her chest, wrapping her arms around her legs. "Not yours either."

He whirled and cast about the room, searching the dresser and nightstand for a useful implement.

"Tools are in the garage," she informed him, a smug smile lifting her cheekbones.

"I'll find something else."

"And do what? How do you know that's not just some kind of portal or something? What if you're not really in the light? You might be in the wall, and without the switch you'd be trapped, wouldn't you? Or you could be in the lamp part," she amended, gesturing to the sconce.

"Doesn't matter."

"Then what? What do you think I should do with the stupid thing? Throw it in the trash and send you off to the landfill?"

Frank snatched a metal nail file from the dresser. "Shut up," he muttered, trying to fit the pointed tip into one of the screws.

"Frank, come on," she cajoled. Her fingers wrapped around his arm, and when he looked down he was nearly blinded by the light emanating from the contact.

"I can't stay here."

"If you do this, we don't know where you'll go. You may be stuck here, or you may end up somewhere else. Do you want to take the chance?"

"Yes."

"Why?"

"Why?" His voice cracked like a teenager's when he repeated the question. "Look at us, Cam!"

"What about us?"

"Look at that," he said, nodding to the pulsing stream of light outlining her fingers.

"Does it hurt?"

He gaped at her, completely thrown by her blasé attitude. "Hurt?"

"Burn or something?" she prompted, tilting her head as she studied the blue-white light.

"Yes," he answered, grasping at any excuse to escape.

"Yes?"

"Yes, it hurts."

Cam let him go, jerking her hand back as if *she* were the one who'd been burned. "I'm sorry."

He stared at the light fixture, her reasoning finally making some sense to him. "I have to figure out how to get out," he muttered.

Cam jerked back. "Being stuck here with me is so bad?"

He turned to face her, gripping the nail file. "Yes."

"I see." She took the file from him, and pinched the handle between her thumb and forefinger, pressing the pointed tip to the center of her palm.

Frank eyed the indention where her skin stretched to give way. She pressed a little harder. "Cam, don't. You're gonna hurt yourself." He made a swipe for the file, but she pulled away.

"What's wrong with me, Frank?"

He searched the depths of her troubled blue eyes. "*Wrong* with you? Nothing's wrong with you."

Cam shook her head. "No. There has to be something wrong."

She swung her legs over the edge of the bed, and he moved, keeping a safe distance between them.

"You told me once you thought I was beautiful," she said quietly. Lifting her gaze to his, she stared at him defiantly. "Other men have told me, too."

His mouth tightened into a grim line, and his hands balled into fists. "Well, there you go. Confirmation."

"But when I want a man..." she continued, "...when I practically *beg* a man to kiss me, touch me, or hell, even fuck me—they tell me no."

"I had to tell you no. I didn't want to. I *had* to," he retorted.

"Why?"

"Why?" He ran his hand over his hair, shaking his head in exasperation. "I'm dead!"

"Not to me, you aren't."

"You need a shrink." Frank blew out a breath. "This isn't real. It isn't healthy, Cam."

"I can't help how I feel about you."

"You need to try. You need to feel this way about someone else. Someone who can give you what you need." The plea in his own voice made him want to cringe, but he stood strong. "I can't be that guy. It's not a matter of not wanting you."

"You aren't the only one," she said flatly.

His jaw ached, the muscle jumping with exertion as he struggled to keep his mouth shut. "*Brad?*" he sneered, failing spectacularly.

A little bubble of surprised laughter burst from her. "How do you know about Brad?"

"You talk in your sleep."

Cam smiled. She had to have caught the jealousy seething in his tone. "Brad doesn't want to kiss me."

Frank's eyes widened then narrowed. "Is he gay?"

"I don't think so."

"Blind?"

"Nope."

Frank snorted. "Castrated?"

Cam arched an eyebrow. "Well, since he won't kiss me, I haven't been able to check."

"You're better off. The guy's obviously nuts."

"Or not interested."

"Not possible."

"Funny that *you* think so."

"Jesus, Cam! I told you, it's never been a question of not wanting to," he hissed. He began to pace the room like a caged animal, which he was in a way. "The guy's home kicking his own ass all over the place for not jumping you when he had the chance," he muttered.

Fire burned in Cam's eyes when they met his. "You had the chance. Lots of chances."

Perhaps the sight of those petal-soft lips parted in anticipation was what spurred him. Maybe the catalyst was the frustration he'd been stewing in since she whispered that name—the name that wasn't his.

It took far too little effort to ignore the tremor in Cam's voice. Frank was almost sorry for her when he yanked her into his arms. He stared into her eyes, needing to be sure she was aware of exactly what she was getting into. Fear flickered in the endless blue depths, striking quick and deadly like a serpent's tongue.

He almost let her go. His brain was issuing the order to his arms at the exact moment she spoke.

"Does it hurt?" she asked in a soft, dangerous whisper.

It wasn't fear *of* him. She was afraid *for* him. Her gaze was alight with concern. Love burned bright, a dancing blue flame that dimmed the blazing current flowing between them.

"Yes. Yes, it hurts," he croaked.

Her breath hitched. The pulse in her throat throbbed. He moved closer, praying for the tingle of her breath against his lips. He waited, concentrating with every ounce of strength he had until he had the answer she didn't dare voice.

His hold on her relaxed, but he kept her close, reveling in the sharp sparks of awareness prickling his skin. "I love you, Cam."

"I love you, too."

"Then let me go."

Her confusion was palpable, every muscle in her body tensed.

"I'm not keeping you here."

"Yes, you are." He opened his eyes. "Give them to me."

"What?"

Impatience and frustration won out. "The books," he managed to grind out between clenched teeth.

Cam stepped back, bracing her hands against his chest to shove him away. "What books?"

A low growl rumbled in his throat. He could tell just by looking at her she knew damn well what he meant. "The diaries, the notebook, give them to me. They can only hurt you. Hurt us both."

She snorted. "They can't hurt me any more than you can."

His temper surged, and he drew back his hand.

Cam's eyes widened then closed to slits when he hesitated. "Go ahead. Show me what a man you are, Frank," she taunted in a whisper.

His hand swung down, his fingers plunging into her hair and tipping her head back. His mouth claimed hers. He pressed his lips to hers in what he hoped was a punishing kiss. They tumbled to the bed. A halo of white light flooded the room, sizzling and shimmering around them as her tongue tangled with his.

Cam arched into him, bucking off of the bed. Her nails scraped over his scalp, scoring it with the urgency of her need.

He ground against her, pressing her into the mattress, desperate to unlock the secret that bound him to her.

Skin. I need her skin. He sent up a fervent prayer. Maybe she could reawaken his senses.

Clawing at the collar of her tee shirt, he curled his fists into the thin fabric and tore it from the neck to the hem.

Cam broke their kiss, gasping her shock. Her chest heaved with exertion and arousal. His didn't move at all.

She wet her lips and he peeled away the remnants of the shirt, exposing her lush, rounded breasts. His hands skimmed the soft indention of her waist, his thumbs meeting as he spanned it with his hands.

"You're perfect," he whispered. "So perfect."

"Oh, Frank..."

His hands slid over stomach, opening to cup her breasts. His thumbs brushed the taut tips of her nipples, and she sucked in a breath as they beaded. He covered the hardened flesh with his palms and squeezed, watching her squirm on the bed beneath him.

"I can't feel you," he rasped, lowering his head to one breast. He drew her nipple into his mouth, suckling deeply as he squeezed the soft mound again.

Cam flinched, wincing in pain, and he froze.

"Oh God," he murmured, almost choking on the words.

He pressed his face to the soft valley between her breasts and collapsed onto her.

"I can't...I can't."

"Shh," she whispered. Her palm smoothed the strip of hair along the center of his head, her caress soothing him.

"I can't taste you," he mumbled against her skin. A tearless sob caught in his throat. "It hurts not to touch you."

"Sh...shh," she crooned, stroking his head, holding him close to her beating heart. "Hush, it's okay. Everything's going to be okay."

"Hurts to touch you and not be able to feel you...to kiss you and not taste you. It's killing me to hold you. I don't get to be the one who keeps on holding you."

He closed his eyes, finding safety in her embrace, trapped in a Hell that burned hotter than a thousand fires.

The room glowed, bathed in the icy moonlight of his skin touching hers. They lay still, arms and legs a tangle, his head pillowed at her bosom. Her hands moved over him, leaving those ghostly trails of sensation. Frank knew in his soul that if he added all those tingling trails together it still wouldn't equal the pleasure of actually feeling her.

Her breathing grew relaxed and even, and her hands slowed their calming caress. He pressed his lips to the curve of her breast and she sighed. For Frank, there was nothing.

He pulled away, disregarding her muffled mewl of protest. Her hand fell from his arm when he climbed from the bed, leaving only the golden pool of lamplight shining over her like the sun. He blinked into the darkness surrounding him, and stared longingly at the ripe curves of her nearly-bare body before his gaze lingered on the carved handle of the nightstand drawer.

"I can't stay here, Cam. You don't know what it's like... Please don't write this. Just let it go. Let me go," he whispered before he left, taking the last of the light with him.

Chapter Ten

Cam felt strangely calm when she awoke the following morning. She showered and dressed as if moving in a fog. After wriggling her feet into her plain black pumps, she sat on the edge of the bed and pulled the notebook she kept as a journal from the nightstand drawer.

She frowned, trying to grasp the thread of what it was she wanted to write down. She flipped to the last page she'd filled. Clicking the plunger on the pen, she turned to a blank page and began writing.

Frank is...scared, petrified.

Brad is...aloof. Or not. Maybe he has his reasons.

I am....

She paused, tapping the pen against her front teeth as she scrambled for the right word. The silence of the house thrummed in her ears. Cam considered and discarded a few choice candidates, then settled on the only one that fit everything she was feeling.

Alone.

Carefully, almost reverently, Cam closed the notebook and put it back in the drawer.

She stood, smoothing her damp palms over the simple black dress she wore. With a tired sigh, she grabbed her cell then headed for the front door.

A car door closed as she slid her key into the deadbolt, and her head popped up. She spotted Brad circling the hood of a gleaming black BMW.

Cam shot the bolt into place and started for the stairs. She cocked her head, taking in the navy suit he wore. The wool was just as expertly tailored as the gray one from the day before, the shirt beneath it was plain, but snowy white. His tie provided the only splash of color.

"Are you going through an Impressionist phase?" she asked, nodding to the pastel water lilies gracefully blurring the silk.

"I thought it was appropriate." He cast a dubious glance at the tie.

"Because you want to make an impression?"

He gave her a weak smile. "Because your dad liked lilies."

His answer brought her up short. Her heels sank into the edge of the lawn as she stared at him. "You're coming today?"

"I told you I would."

"Yeah, but, I thought you meant last night..." She bit her lip as she met his steady gaze. "Last night didn't go so well."

"Today is a new day." He opened the passenger door. "I thought we could ride together."

Cam turned to look at her dilapidated, old Chevy. "You don't want to ride in my car?"

"Not on a bet."

She couldn't help it; she had to laugh. "Snob," she teased, easing herself into the buttery-soft leather seat.

"Yeah, I am."

The car door closed without the screech of over-taxed hinges, and she chuckled again as Brad made his way to the driver's side.

"I wasn't going to take it to the cemetery."

He backed out of the drive. "This way you don't have to jockey for the Buick."

"I wasn't taking the Buick either. The funeral home has a Town Car. I was going to follow...uh, them to the cemetery."

Brad nodded. "Okay, we can do that."

Beneath the shining hood the engine purred, its dulcet tones only giving way to a guttural Germanic growl when he pulled away from the stop sign. Brad's hands tightened on the wheel as he slowed at a stop light.

He stared straight ahead, his voice strained, "I wanted to kiss you last night, just so we're clear."

"My mother's name was Lily Rose," she blurted at the same time.

Their eyes met, and they both chuckled.

"Back to taking numbers," Cam murmured. "Why didn't you?"

"That's a pretty name," he said simultaneously.

Cam laughed and pressed her fingertip to his lips. He pursed them slightly, pressing them to the pad of her finger. "It's okay," she whispered as she drew her hand away.

She noticed the light had changed, but Brad was still staring at her. "Green light," she prompted, gesturing to the intersection. The tires hummed against asphalt, and she sank into the leather cocoon surrounding her. "This is a nice car. Now that I'm an heiress and all, I might buy one."

"It would be good if you got something where your feet didn't go through the floorboard like Fred Flintstone."

Cam grinned. "Aw, are you worried about me?"

"Yes."

Startled by his blunt answer, she turned to study him. "You are?"

"Yeah. Is that surprising?"

"A little," she admitted. "You hardly know me."

"I know cars, and yours is a death wish."

"How appropriate, since we're going to a funeral," she quipped.

"Don't say that," he grumbled in response.

"Wow, someone's a little sensitive. It's my father who died, not yours."

"I hate it when people treat life like it's some kind of a joke."

"You think I do that?"

"I think you use jokes to avoid dealing with things."

"Such an astute observation for a man who doesn't know my middle name," she said in a taut voice.

"Some things are easy to figure out," he muttered, signaling the turn into the parking lot. He pulled to a stop near the portico, parking his car behind the hearse and the waiting Town Car.

He pinned her with those grass-green eyes. "I couldn't kiss you last night. Not like that. I was scared you'd get it all mixed up with this," he said, waving a hand at the waiting hearse.

"That makes no sense."

He rubbed a hand over his face then stared through the windshield. "Maybe it doesn't...I don't know." Turning back to her, Brad gave her a tired smile. "The point is I want to know your middle name. I want to know how much ketchup you use, and what shoe size you wear. I want to know what makes you happy, truly happy, and I think I might want to be the guy who gives it to you."

"In much of a rush?" she asked, breathless.

He gestured to the funeral parlor. "Life is short."

She bristled. "Now who's making bad jokes?"

"I'm not joking. I know what I want."

"What do you want from me?" she asked, frustration edging her voice.

Brad laughed, and reached for her hand. He held hers between both of his, brushing his thumb across her knuckles. "Probably too much, too soon," he admitted. "I just.... Let me be here for you. Give me a chance to get to know you. Give me a shot at being the guy."

Cam's heart hammered in her chest, thudding against the confines of her breastbone. Unable to bear the intensity of his gaze, she lowered her eyes, watching him stroke her skin with his thumb.

"Rose," she whispered. "My middle name is Rose too."

He smiled and pulled her hand to his lips, brushing the barest of kisses to the spot his thumb had claimed moments before. Her fingers slid from his when he reached for the door handle. "Someday I'll tell you mine," he promised, giving Cam a broad wink.

****

They sent Tom Haskell and Marjorie ahead in the Town Car. By the time they reached the cemetery, she'd wheedled an initial out of Brad.

"Edgar? Elliott?" she guessed, clinging to his arm as they crossed the lawn.

A blue awning snapped in the brisk spring wind. The casket stood graveside. A blanket of snowy lilies and roses gleamed in the weak sunshine. Brad slowed a little and brushed the hair clinging to her lip gloss away from her cheek. "No."

****

"Ewen?" she whispered as the minister opened his Bible.

"Nuh uh," he grunted, covering the hand that gripped his sleeve.

****

Cam clutched the top of the open car door with the hand holding a crumpled tissue. "Elton?" she asked, her voice cracking.

"Not even close," he answered, ushering her into the car.

****

Brad pulled to a stop in her driveway and killed the engine. Cam fidgeted with her purse strap. "Are you sure you don't want me to take you somewhere else?"

"Where?"

Her question made him pause. "I could take you to work with me," he suggested at last.

Cam favored him with a wan smile. "You don't need to worry about me. I've been taking care of myself for a long time."

He chuckled and said, "You aren't old enough to say that."

"I was the woman of the house when I was six."

"Cam..."

"Egbert? Eli? Emmanuel?"

"Camellia Rose," he murmured, capturing a lock of her hair between his fingers.

"Stop trying to distract me, Bradley Emeril."

"Bam!" he whispered.

"Am I close?"

"Not at all."

"Thank you for today. And yesterday," she added. Her fingers curled into the soft leather of her purse as his slipped from her hair.

"Although I liked your dad, I admit my motives are not completely selfless."

Her gaze fell to the purse clutched on her lap. "I don't care what they are."

"You have my number, right? Call me if you want to talk."

"I will."

She reached for the door handle, but he put his hand on her arm.

"I'll do that," he said, bailing from the car.

Brad opened her door, and Cam looked up at him with an amused smile. "I can handle a door." She slid from the seat and stood in front of him.

"I don't doubt that for a minute." He stepped back to allow her to pass. "I'm pretty sure you can handle anything."

"You think?"

He nodded. "I'm the one who's a little off-kilter."

Cam smiled, peeking at him from under her lashes as she inched past him. "Good."

She pulled her house keys from her purse. "See you later, Bradley Ezra."

"See you tomorrow, Camellia Rose," he corrected, meeting her eyes.

"Tomorrow," she confirmed and turned toward the house.

She hurried up the steps, acutely aware he was watching her. She slid the key into the lock and glanced over her shoulder. Brad leaned against the car, his arms crossed over his chest, one ankle propped over the other.

"Go to work!" she called, shooing him away with a wave of her hand.

He flashed a slow, devastating smile. "I will. Eventually."

Cam rolled her eyes and pushed through the door. After closing it behind her, she collapsed against the smooth wood, waiting until she heard the purr of the engine. Then she dashed to the front window like a lovesick teenager and watched the immaculate black car glide away.

She tossed her purse onto the couch and wandered to the stereo, tuning to the soft-rock station. Padding down the hall, she spotted the clothes strewn across her bedroom floor. Cam wrinkled her nose and turned away.

She stared at the closed door to her mother's office. Her fingers closed around the cut-glass knob. The latch gave way without a squeak. The door swung open in invitation. She stepped into the room, releasing the air held captive in her lungs.

Cam sank into the old-fashioned desk chair and ran a finger along a file cabinet. She wasn't surprised when she failed to gather a speck of dust. A quick tug on the handle, and the drawer opened, moving easily on well-oiled rollers.

A manila file folder labeled 'IDEAS' poked out above the others, practically begging her to choose it, so she did. As she placed it in the center of the blotter, a sob strangled her vocal cords, choking off the moan of pain that rose when she recognized her mother's loopy handwriting.

Biting her lip, she scanned the scribbles, uncertain of what she was looking for, but positive she'd find what she needed on the page. Scrawled across the second-to-last line she spotted something that spoke to her.

'Crawdad Corner—A village, or a small southern town. Crazy characters. A little magic? A girl crawdad with the strongest pincers in town? Maybe she becomes the bodyguard to the embattled Crawdad King?'

A flash of memory flickered to life. Lily crouched beside her at the creek bed, her dark hair spilling over her shoulder as she gingerly lifted a crayfish from the muddied water.

"Look at his pincers. They're very strong." Her mother *pulled the crawdad away when Cam reached for the slimy little creature. "Careful, he could hurt you."*

She turned the crawfish so Cam could have a better look at it. "He has a shell. That's his suit of armor. I bet he's a knight."

"Or a king," Cam lisped in an awed tone.

"Perhaps," Lily *conceded. "Or he's the knight who protects his king,"* she murmured, *eying the specimen speculatively.*

Gently, she put the crawdad back in the cool water. "Come on, my precious flower. Daddy will be home soon, and he'll be hungry enough to eat a horse."

Cam blinked back tears, pressing the open file folder to her chest. She stared at the ceiling, focusing on each breath she took. A month after the outing to the creek, her mother was dead. Cam had stumbled off the school bus and was intercepted by Mrs. Kelly. The house was filled with people—friends, neighbors, people who worked with her father, but Cam stood alone in the entryway.

Her daddy sat in the chair in the corner, his tie askew, his hair mussed by his own hands. He looked up and spotted her. The room fell silent. He stared at Cam, his mouth moving, but no sound came out. He opened his arms and she ran to him, climbing into his lap and clinging to his neck.

She didn't understand what was happening. Her mother wasn't home to meet her, and too many people were in her house. They began to talk again, whispering in low, worried voices. Her father held her tight, his tears seeping through her striped shirt, his chest shaking with barely suppressed sobs.

"My flower. My precious flower," he murmured, stroking her hair blindly.

He wasn't talking to her. Somehow Cam was aware she wasn't the one who needed comfort. Smoothing his rumpled hair with her tiny hands, she whispered to him, crooning the words her mother used when she scraped a knee or broke a toy.

"Sh...shh. It's okay. Everything's gonna be okay, Daddy."

Cam tipped back in the chair, tears trailing down her temples, and soaking into her hair. She let them flow, focusing her gaze on a brown water stain in the corner of the ceiling. When they slowed, she leaned forward, mopping her face with the heels of her hands.

She laid the folder in the center of the desk, and rummaged through the center drawer for a pencil. Nodding, she pressed it to the paper, comforted by the rasp of graphite against compressed wood pulp.

"Claudius," she whispered. "The king's name would be Claudius. Our hero's a boy. His name is Pete. Peter Pincer. Sound good, Mommy?"

Chapter Eleven

Brad tried to keep busy, but as the evening wore down he knew he was failing. Unless sitting at his breakfast bar staring at the digital display of the microwave could be considered busy. In that case, he was swamped.

He'd done better earlier, but that wasn't saying much. The moment he reached the office that afternoon, he plunged headlong into work, trying to catch up on everything he'd neglected since Camellia Stafford rocked his world Tuesday morning. Of course, he'd been distracted. A sketch of Cam's lips now graced the folder holding the pitch for a snack-food manufacturer. A line drawing of her sinuous curves decorated the margin of a report one of the account managers had left in his inbox.

Only two days had passed since Camellia Stafford stepped onto her back porch and demanded to know what he was doing in her yard. *Ogled me openly then demanded to know what I was doing in her yard*, he amended with a smug smile. Brad took another sip of his beer.

He was aware two days wasn't very much time, but just the same, his attraction to her had sparked long ago. It was possible the pull she held over him harkened back to the day she'd caught him spurting the garden hose while ogling *her*. For a moment, he worried that the fact she even spoke to him might just be some elaborate ogling payback scheme.

He knew it wasn't. Just like he knew his fascination with Camellia Stafford didn't begin the day she climbed out of her wreck of a car.

One day long ago, he'd spotted her studying his scholarship-winning charcoal drawing in the high school lobby. Cam stared at the picture intently, oblivious to the gushing flow of jostling bodies around her. When she leaned forward, a curtain of spiraling goldenrod curls shielded her cheek. He remembered the way she flipped her hair over her shoulder. A gesture that was now groin-tighteningly familiar.

Two of her friends approached, pulling her toward the cafeteria. Her gaze flitted over him and landed on the drawing again. He'd watched her go, swamped by the overwhelming urge to chase after her, wanting to know if it was the interruption that drew her eyebrows together in a scowl of annoyance, or something she spotted in the drawing that no one else, not even the judges, had seen.

Brad shook off the memory and reached for his beer, surreptitiously checking the time again. He'd stayed late at the office, hoping the time would pass faster if he kept busy. It didn't. He still had eight minutes, and every one of them threatened to stretch interminably. Now, he was busy sitting at his breakfast bar staring at the clock on his microwave.

He laughed at his own pathos, picked up his bottle of beer, and drained it. Tipping the bottle cap on its edge, he flicked it with his middle finger and the spinning top careened toward the lip of the counter. It took the plunge, clattering to the tiled floor with a strangely satisfying clatter.

Brad checked the clock once more, and decided it was close enough. He was out the door in seconds, his bare feet pounding the cool concrete walkway. Impatient, he cut across the grass, dodged the fence post marking the Kelly's property, and trotted along the sidewalk.

He drew to a halt beside her car and pressed one hand to the hood. The chilled metal told him she hadn't gone anywhere in the past hour or two. He craned his neck and took a few steps along the drive. The kitchen lights still burned brightly. Brad spotted the glow of another light peeping through the crack in the picture window's draperies.

"Stalker," he muttered under his breath. "Peeping Brad."

He jogged up the porch steps, rapped his knuckles against the door, and stood back, burying his hands in the pockets of his paint-stained jeans. A full minute passed. He was about to give up and go home when he heard her shuffling toward the door.

She opened it a crack, one bleary blue eye appearing in the space the old-fashioned chain lock allowed. "Oh. Hi."

"Hey," he exhaled.

Cam promptly closed the door. For a split second, he almost panicked. Then he heard the rustle of the chain.

She opened the door wider, a sheepish smile curving her lips as she smoothed the sharp creases that cut across the rumpled black dress she'd worn that morning. "Hi."

His gaze swept from her bare toes to the bundle of hair held in place with two sharpened pencils. "Are you okay?"

Her smile was slow to blossom, but soon suffused her face, lighting her eyes with blue flames. Brad took an involuntary step back, stunned by the transformation. Then he moved forward, drawn like a moth.

"I'm *great*."

"Great?" He couldn't keep his puzzlement from his voice. He had expected any number of greetings, but not this one.

"Fabulous," she confirmed. She hugged herself, shivering in the cool night air. "Are *you* okay?"

He raised his wrist to double-check his watch, needing to be sure he wasn't going back on his word. The minute hand moved another tick past the twelve and he nodded emphatically. "It's tomorrow."

"What?"

"Now. It's past midnight. Tomorrow. Or today," he rambled, closing the distance between them.

Cam gaped at him, tipping her head back as his hand settled on her waist. "Huh?"

"A brand new day," he murmured, lowering his lips to hers.

It took a moment for her to catch on, but Cam rose on her toes to prolong the kiss. His fingers flexed, digging into the sweet curve of her hip, drawing her closer to him.

She came willingly, pressing her body to his. Her hands locked at the nape of his neck, her fingers slid into his hair, and a tingle tripped down his spine when her nails raked his scalp.

"Earl?" she whispered when they parted.

Her breath tickled his lips. "No," he breathed, capturing her mouth again.

He might have moaned, or maybe it was her. It didn't matter. All that mattered was the soft cushion of her mouth against his. A faint whiff of chocolate teased his nostrils. Sugar lingered on her lips. Sugar and...something else. His mind raced, running through his sensory catalog until he struck gold. Milk. She'd been drinking milk.

She pulled back, and he couldn't resist brushing his thumb over her full bottom lip. "You taste like milk and cookies."

"They were some snickerdoodles left over. I had them for dinner," she confessed. Her impish grin made the dimple in her cheek flash.

He dipped his head and inhaled deeply, drinking in the scent of fruity shampoo and lavender scented lotion. He kissed her again, drawing her deeper, capturing her bottom lip between his and sucking gently. A granule of sugar melted in his mouth, making his head spin.

They stumbled into the foyer in a tangle of arms and legs. Cam laughed when they broke apart, and he bent his head again, capturing the joyful sound with a sweet kiss.

"I couldn't wait," he confessed.

Cam's fingers curled in his shirt and she took a step back, urging him closer still until she bumped into the wall. "I'm glad."

He took a wild swing at the door and somehow connected. When he didn't hear the latch catch, he kicked out, nearly toppling them over. He ignored the jolt of pain shooting from his toes to his ankle, letting the sound of Cam's laughter vibrate through him.

His fingers threaded into her hair. The pencils fell to the floor. Silky waves of amber cascaded over his wrists, gleaming in the dim light from the hall. "You're okay?"

"I'm fine."

"You're beautiful."

"Your vision is wonky. You must be in your Dali phase."

"I hated leaving you here."

She smiled and pressed her hand to his cheek. "You're sweet."

Instinctively, he leaned into her caress. "No, I'm not."

"No, not at all," she crooned.

Her teasing tone set fire to the embers burning low and insistent in his gut. Her hand fell to his arm, grasping his bicep for balance when he captured her lips in a blazing kiss. His tongue traced the seam of her lips, and she fisted the sleeve of his tee shirt. Her head hit the wall when she parted her lips, but neither of them noticed.

His tongue touched hers, stoking the fire, setting his senses ablaze. His blood pulsed through his veins, molten but sluggish. When his hands molded to her ribcage, he felt the thud of her heart. The wrinkled linen of her dress bunched as they slid higher, grazing her breasts. Their tongues tangled and knotted around one another's in a heated battle.

She wouldn't win. She couldn't win. He'd wanted her too long; he needed her too badly.

Brad ground against her, barely clinging to a sliver of control as her lush, ripe curves cushioned his body in blessed femininity. His blood sang in his veins, drowning out all reasonable thought and smothering the best of his intentions.

A framed photograph crashed to the floor at their feet. He pulled back, his chest heaving as he stared into her bewildered eyes. Somehow they'd made it to the hallway leading to the bedrooms. Biting his lip to clamp down on the need clawing at him, he stroked her cheek tenderly, needing to soothe the abrasions his stubble left behind.

"I just wanted to kiss you."

Her answering smile told him she didn't buy his lie. Her kiss-swollen lips tantalized him, the promise they held making his body scream for release.

"I just want you to kiss me some more," she whispered.

A white-hot spear of lust shot through him like a bolt of lightning. He lips sought hers again. Brad held her head in his hands, trapping her while his lips, teeth, and tongue plundered her mouth. Cam moaned, low in her throat. The arch of her foot brushed the back of his leg. She squirmed and surged against him.

His heart beat a stuttering tattoo. At any other time, in any other place, the staccato pace might have worried him. Here, holding her in his arms, he didn't give a damn if he dropped dead on the spot as long as he could taste her on his lips.

He was free—released from the bonds of his self-imposed restraint and a lifetime of caution. Free to kiss her as much as he needed to, and at the moment he needed to kiss her more than he needed his heart to keep beating.

Cam whimpered, circling her hips against his, her foot pressing into his calf muscle. She broke the kiss, whispering a fervent, "Please," into his ear.

He shivered, her warm, moist breath shooting arrows of sensation straight to his groin. Her leg jerked, straining against the confines of her dress. The source of her distress finally seeped into his muddled brain.

Lowering his lips to her throat, his teeth scraped against her skin. He grasped her leg, his fingers stroking the sweet spot behind her knee before sliding up to cradle the back of her thigh.

He made a mental note to pay more attention to that particular spot later, when the need to hike her skirt over her satiny skin wasn't tearing him to shreds. He nipped at her ear lobe, subtle payback for the torment her writhing was causing him. "Cam," he panted, his voice as ragged as his breathing.

"Please. Oh, please..."

Her plea snapped what little control he had left. Too far gone for finesse, he pushed the skirt up roughly and ran the tip of one finger along the elastic of her panties. She hooked her leg over his, holding him to her.

The heat of her arousal soaked through the layers of fabric. His knuckles grazed the slippery fabric covering her sex. A hot rush of power pulsed through his body.

"Let me be the guy, Camellia," he whispered.

Her eyelashes fluttered. She blinked at him, the movement lazy and languid, seeming to take hours. Her vivid blue eyes had turned smoky and hazy with desire.

"I want to be the guy who gives you what you want."

"You," she exhaled.

"Me. Let me be the man who gives you what you need."

"Brad..."

The sound of his name tumbling from her kiss-swollen lips sealed his fate. His body ached with need. His soul screamed for her.

Pinning her to the wall, he covered her breast with one hand. Her heart hammered under his fingers, the soft mound filled his palm. Her nipples rose, begging for his attention. Her hips bucked against his other hand, seeking his touch. The certainty of her desire consumed him. His fingers slipped under the elastic and filled her with one powerful stroke.

Cam cried out, her nails biting into his shoulder. He drove into her, the heel of his hand stroking her sensitive flesh. She was scorching hot, her body tight and demanding, closing around his fingers and dragging him deeper.

Her eyes widened and her nostrils flared. He stood transfixed, utterly absorbed in the play of pleasure on her features. His brain pinged as the scent of her desire enveloped them. Brilliant brushstrokes swished through his mind—creamy white skin flushed rose pink, the stark darkness of her dress contrasting sharply with the pale swell of her breast peeking above the neckline as he cupped her. He'd paint her knuckles white as bone where she clung to him, her lips ruby red where they parted. The image of Cam climaxing etched into his brain. He would call it *Surrender.*

His. He wanted to make her his in every way.

The soul-shattering certainty of his desire rocked him back on his heels as she slumped against the wall. He stared at her, stunned by the intensity of the emotion swirling inside of him. He needed her—heart, body, and soul.

Gathering her into his arms, he held her tight. Her soft, slumberous chuckle was muffled by his shirt, but the rumble of her laugh vibrated against him.

"Sorry, been a while," she murmured, pressing a distracted kiss to his throat.

Pride surged through his veins making him nearly giddy. A short, sharp laugh depleted the last of his oxygen supply. He buried his face in her hair, inhaling the faint, fruity scent of her shampoo as if the fragrance could restore sanity.

His voice came rough and low, almost unrecognizable to his own ears. "Good."

Cam laughed. Her eyes crinkled at the corners, twinkling at him when she pulled back. "I could just be a little pent up, you know."

He shook his head, smoothing her hair back from her face and gathering the tousled waves in his hands. "Don't say that," he whispered. "Don't break my heart."

She looked into his eyes, blinking as if she were trying to battle her way through the haze of pleasure shrouding her mind. A sharp stab of alarm pierced his heart. He didn't want her to think. He didn't want her clear-headed. He wanted her to feel. Brad needed her as irrational as he was, so he did the only thing he could do to thwart reason.

Parting her lips with his tongue, he drew hers into his mouth with deep, drugging pulls. His hands moved restlessly over her body, smoothing the rumpled fabric of her dress and gathering it again, impatient with the barrier keeping her from him. He pushed the skirt to her waist, and cupped the rounded curves of her buttocks, urging her closer to him.

Cam whimpered softly, and he chose to interpret that as a yes. His hands slid to her thighs, and he broke the kiss, stooping to lift her.

She wrapped her legs around his waist and his knees almost buckled. Her arms draped lazily over his shoulders, her face was buried in his neck. Her sweet whimper turned to a throaty laugh. Her body shook when he pressed her against the wall to shift her weight. He didn't know if it was amusement or arousal, and either way, he couldn't have cared less.

With her lush bottom cradled in his palms, he pushed away, careening down the hall. Another picture was knocked askew, and he delivered his most heart-felt apology in a kiss. She kissed him back, giving as good as she got while he ricocheted off the frame of the bathroom door. By the time they reached her bedroom, he'd gained the upper hand again by laving the pulse pounding in her throat with his tongue.

"Jesus, you taste as good as you look," he rasped against her ear.

Cam laughed and slipped her hands under the hem of his shirt. She pressed them into his back, her breath coming in short, sharp puffs against his ear. "You feel better than I imagined."

He chuckled, and the pulse in her throat jumped. He drew her skin into his mouth, suckling gently, drinking in his reward.

"Imagined, huh? Have you thought about me, Cam?" he murmured, raining soft kisses along her jaw. She hummed distractedly. "God, I've thought about you." A shiver danced along her spine and he chased the tremor with his fingertips. "All I could think about was you."

"Brad..."

He cut her off with a kiss, desperate to keep her from thinking about anything but him.

"I drew you," he confessed, raking his fingers through her hair and tilting her head back. "I tried to work, but all I saw was you. I tried to think, but all I could think about was you."

Her response to his admission was instantaneous and insistent. She jerked his shirt up, bunching it at his shoulders. Reluctantly he released her, allowing her to strip the barrier over his head and toss it aside.

He held his breath when she spread her hands over his chest. Her touch was proprietary. Cam's thumbs teased his nipples as they trailed lower. One delicate finger slid under the waistband of his jeans, and the air exploded from his lungs.

He gasped for precious oxygen when the button popped open. For a crazed moment, he wondered if it was her doing, or if the sheer force of his throbbing erection was answering her unspoken request. He stood mesmerized by the sight of her slender fingers toying with the hair on his stomach; his heart threatened to leap from his chest. He tried to speak, but no words came out.

"I want you naked," she said in a bold, breathy whisper.

Thinking and talking seemed vastly overrated. With numbed fingers, he found the tab of her zipper. In one pull, her back was bared to the waist. His hand glided over her satin skin and he pulled her close, pressing her cheek to his shoulder.

"You're killing me," he rasped. The clasp of her bra sprung open, and tension coiled in his gut like a spring.

Her lips curved against his skin. "I take it you want me naked, too."

When she stepped away, he dragged her dress over her shoulders, trapping her arms against her sides. His gaze fell to the tantalizing jut of her collarbone. On impulse he bent forward, pressing his lips to the sweet, vulnerable skin at the hollow of her throat.

"If I had my way, you'd never wear clothes again," he growled against her neck, peeling her dress and bra from her body.

"I'd get cold," she whispered.

"I'll keep you warm."

It wasn't an empty promise. Heat radiated from his skin as her dress pooled at their feet. Brad dragged her to him, groaning when her breasts flattened against his chest. He caressed her bottom, enjoying the juxtaposition of the satiny-slick fabric against the smooth velvet of her skin.

The fascination didn't last long. Velvet won, hands down, and *his* hands were down her panties before his brain even registered the thought. They fell to her feet.

She clutched his forearm and stepped out of them. Cam tossed her hair over her shoulder. When she looked at him, the hint of a small smile teased the corners of her mouth.

Unable to resist the challenge, Brad pressed one hand to her back, plastering her against his chest as he began moving toward the bed. When the backs of her knees nudged the mattress, he took her hands in his, imprisoning them in a vise-like grip and raising them over her head.

He kissed her, pouring every ounce of pent-up passion into her. She sank to the bed and took him with her. Loose-limbed and languid, she stretched out and reached for the headboard, their fingers still enmeshed.

He planted one knee between her legs and brought the other beside her thigh, looming over her. Her fingers curled around his, holding him captive. He pressed her hands into the pillow, torn between giving in to the urge to tumble on top of her and the need to see all of her, touch every inch of her.

He gave her hands an impatient tug. "Let me go."

Cam sucked in a breath, gasping as if he'd punched her. She released him so abruptly he almost fell onto her. With a low chuckle he rocked back, but the laughter died on his lips when he registered the stricken look on her face.

Puzzled, he reached up to stroke her cheek. "Is this okay? Do you want me to stop?"

Cam bit her lip and closed her eyes. "No, don't stop." She pressed her hands to the headboard, offering herself to him.

Brad caressed the swell of her stomach reverently, attempting to memorize her with his hands. Her eyes remained closed, but she bowed from the bed, urging his exploration.

"Are you sure?"

"I'm sure."

"I don't want to push you."

"I want you to..."

"I want to touch you. I need to feel you."

He cupped her breasts, testing their weight in his palms, his thumbs teasing the beaded tips. Pink as a flower petal, her body responded instantly to his demands.

"Camellia Rose," he whispered, needing her to open her eyes.

She moaned as he pinched one taut nipple, rolling it between his thumb and forefinger. He lowered his mouth to her, lavishing attention on the afflicted flesh with the flat of his tongue, then drawing it into his mouth insistently.

His kisses rained over her in the dim light that streaked from the hall into her room. It wasn't enough. He wasn't sure he'd ever have enough. He wanted to paint her in sunlight, sketch her in shade. He needed his hands on her in the dark of night, sculpting her curves, shaping them with his fingers and cupping them in his palms.

When he raised his head, she gasped—an inarticulate grunt of protest. A rueful laugh shook his body and he swiveled his head, checking the nightstand for a lamp.

Cam opened her eyes just as he spotted the wall sconce. He stretched, grappling with the switch. A desperate squeak of protest caught in her throat, and she clutched his arm to stop him.

He shook his head as a warm spill of honeyed light illuminated them, baring them to one another. She crossed an arm over her breasts, his name rushing from her lips.

Brad just smiled, gently removing her arm and pinning it firmly above her head. "Don't hide. You're beautiful, Camellia." His fingers chased the light over every delicious dip and curve of her. "You are the most beautiful woman I've ever seen."

Chapter Twelve

Melted? Sappy? Both were perfectly good words, but Cam rejected each of them as she stretched toward the headboard, taking Brad with her. The only apt descriptor her befuddled brain grasped was 'gooey,' and as a writer, she rejected it too.

Brad.

She clung to his hands as his name echoed in her head, bouncing off her skull, pounding its way into every thought she'd ever had. This was the Brad she wanted to know. This strange mix of the intense, determined man in ruthlessly tailored suits, the devastating flirt who moved with disconcerting grace in shorts that sagged from his sweat-sheened body, and the easy, affable neighbor who wore soft, faded jeans and drew pictures of mice dressed as knights.

When she opened the door to find him on her porch, she'd almost jumped him on sight. It might have been the washed-thin tee shirt that clung to his broad shoulders. The faded, frayed, paint-spattered jeans forming to the long, lean muscles of his thighs might have been a factor.

The endearing sight of him rubbing one bare foot against the top of the other to warm it didn't hurt, nor did the genuine worry in his voice. She would have kissed him for those things alone, but what sealed her fate were his emerald eyes—sparkling with determination, and glimmering with greed the moment he saw her.

He wanted her. He wanted her, and she wanted him. It was basic, an autonomic response as natural as breathing out and breathing in and as unavoidable as blinking.

He had reduced her to this—to feeling gooey each time his lips touched hers.

He kissed her and she was lost. He kept kissing her, and the yearning ache inside of her whispered maybe she had found her way home.

His kisses were mind-numbing, laced with opiate, and tinged with something which defied definition. His graceful, talented fingers stroked her until her blood ran so thick and hot she wondered how it moved through her veins. When his teeth sank into her ear lobe, she didn't care if it flowed or not.

His tongue traced the shell of her ear and she shivered as the word burst through the slumberous haze of desire.

Quicksilver.

The perfect word. In his hands she was Mercury—tensile, but delicate. The heat of their kisses sent her soaring. She clutched his back, fusing him to her. His denim-clad thighs bracketed one of hers in an iron grip, and she turned to liquid. Her bones were dense and heavy, but fluid. Her fingers tightened on his in a vain attempt to make her churning emotions seep into his skin.

Brad tried to pull his hands from hers, but she held fast.

He chuckled, mocking her token resistance. "Let me go."

His words twisted like a knife in her gut. She automatically released him. He laughed and shifted away from her, but Cam's eyes stayed fixed on him confused by her own reaction.

When he met her gaze, his laughter died. A tiny furrow of worry bisected his eyebrows. His fingers stroked her cheek. "I want to touch you. I need to feel you."

The surge of relief that coursed through her was so intense she nearly cried out. She bit her lip and closed her eyes, hoping he hadn't seen the desperation in them. Anxious to ensnare him again, she pressed her hands to the headboard, silently signaling her capitulation.

His hands were on her again, adding fuel to the fire that burned low and insistent deep inside. The aged wood of the headboard was smooth under her palms. She was grounded, elemental, as if being loved by him was what she was meant for. He cupped her breasts and she arched her back, giving their full, ripe weight over to him.

"Camellia Rose," he whispered.

He caught her nipple between his thumb and fore-finger and a low, urgent moan roared from the flames leaping inside of her. His narcotic lips closed around her aching flesh, and his tongue soothed her. The insistent pull of his mouth was a speedball. Her bones liquefied and her blood raced. Bolts of sensation careened to all points south.

She wanted to touch him as he touched her. She wanted to memorize the lean sweep of his muscles, to conquer the broad expanse of his shoulders, lay claim to his narrow hips, and plunge her hands into the gaping waistband of his jeans.

She couldn't. It was all she could do to press her hands into the unyielding wood of the headboard, bracing herself against the torrent of need he unleashed in her.

Desire roiled in her belly. Her fingers itched for him. They wanted to dance along the long length of his spine. Unable to bear it a moment longer, she was about to reach for him when he raised his head—abandoning her when she needed him most.

An unladylike grunt burst from her lips and she opened her eyes, shooting him an indignant glare. He didn't notice because he was too busy squinting into the darkness of the room. He rose, and she saw his long arm reaching for the switch on the wall lamp. Cam clutched at his bicep, choking on the warning she was compelled to call out.

A pool of golden light enveloped them. Instinctively, she covered her breasts with her arm and gasped, "Brad..."

Brad begged her not to hide from him. He told her she was beautiful and the hitch in his voice was enough to make her believe him. She exhaled, absorbing his words, letting them leach into her skin. His fingers traced the shape of her body, and hers curled reflexively into her palm. His hands slid over her hips and he whispered the words every woman yearned to hear.

She sighed, her heavy eyelids closing as he brushed a kiss to the valley between her breasts. She was quicksilver, reflecting the golden light that shone over them. In his hands, she was his truth—the most beautiful woman in the world.

"He's right. You're hot, Cam," Frank said tersely.

Her eyes flew open as Brad's lips claimed her nipple once more. He interpreted her cry of distress as one of desire, and pulled her deeper into his mouth.

The inarticulate squeaks coming from her throat seemed to inflame Brad as much as they amused Frank, but they only served to infuriate her. Cam cradled the back of Brad's head, holding him to her breast. She flailed her free hand, trying in vain to shoo Frank from the room.

Frank's answering smile was cold and brittle. "Hell no, I'm stayin' for the show."

He planted his feet in a wide stance and crossed his arms over the Metallica logo, glaring at them from the foot of the bed.

Brad shifted to her other breast. His teeth abraded the hard tip of her nipple, and she gasped.

Frank moved closer, glowering at the back of Brad's head. "Tastes as good as she looks, huh? You're a regular fucking poet, buddy."

"Stop," Cam hissed between clenched teeth.

Brad's head jerked up. "I'm sorry. Did I hurt you?"

The tip of his tongue brushed her swollen nipple, soothing her with its sweet caress. Cam's blood surged. Lust, anger, and confusion churned through her as the engorged tip swelled, pouting for more.

"Sorry," she panted. Cupping the nape of his neck, she locked eyes with Frank as she pulled Brad to her breast again.

Brad showered her skin with tiny kisses. "Do you want me to stop?"

"You don't, do you, Cam?" Frank said in a low, taunting voice.

The ache in Brad's voice ripped at her. The challenge in Frank's dark eyes made her blood boil. "No."

Brad blazed a trail of soft, wet kisses over the top of her breast then nuzzled the tender underside. "You were made for this," he murmured. "For me...."

Frank snorted. "Not hardly, pal."

Brad covered her stomach with sweet, sucking, open-mouthed kisses. He moved lower, painting her skin in delicate brushstrokes with his tongue. His hands stroked the hollows of her hips, teasing the tops of her thighs until her legs parted.

A low groan filled the room, and Cam clamped her mouth shut. It wasn't until Frank moved into her line of vision that she realized it had come from him, and not her. His lips were damp and parted, his gaze fixed on Brad's dark head nuzzling the curls covering her sex.

"A goddess," Brad murmured. His fingers whispering along the insides of her thighs. "Marble, not bronze."

Tripping, tumbling, her heart stumbled in her chest. She stared at his glossy dark hair, picking up the elusive hints of russet winking in the soft, golden glow.

Her gaze jerked to Frank when he grunted. "Marble's too hard. Cam is soft."

She moaned and a hot, wet rush of sensation pooled between her parted legs. In a silent plea, Cam raised her hips, staring at Frank as she clutched the faded comforter in her fists.

"I want it to be me," Frank said, meeting her fevered gaze.

"Alabaster," Brad whispered, his hot breath stirring the soft curls. "Rose alabaster." His tongue dipped into her folds, making her cry out again.

"Pink and perfect. Sweet? Is she sweet?" Frank asked Brad.

A rush of panic flooded her, but it was obvious Brad didn't hear him.

"Make her come. I want her to come," Frank whispered.

"No!" she panted.

"God, yes," Brad answered, the blunt tips of his fingers digging into her thighs as he pressed his eager mouth to her wet folds.

She nearly bolted from the bed. The heat of his tongue seared her, every nerve ending in her body stood at attention. Her fingers sank into Brad's hair, holding him close but all the while squirming away from his questing tongue.

"Hot, sweet. I bet you taste like honey," Frank murmured. "Christ, Cam, you're so wet."

"Stop! Stop!"

Brad groaned and set out on a quest to change her mind. His lips brushed her thigh and she quivered. "Please, Cam…"

"Please, Cam, let him," Frank whispered, his voice taut and strained.

"But…"

"I want you," Brad said, meeting her gaze directly.

She trembled, her thighs quaking in Brad's hands, her body seizing as a contraction of pleasure tore through her. Brad groaned, thrusting his tongue into her again.

"I want to kiss you. I want you," Frank murmured.

The envy in his voice set off another ripple of ecstasy. Her mind splintered, shattering into a thousand pieces that somehow fit together like the shifting shapes of a kaleidoscope.

Brad thrust his fingers into her as she began to spasm, grounding her in the here and now. Colors danced behind her eyelids, but no words. For a moment, she feared she'd never find the words again.

"I'll never taste you. I'll never touch you. I could bury myself inside of you, and I wouldn't feel you," Frank continued. "I can't, Cam."

She shuddered, her arms and legs jerking as each flash of fire licked at her. Stirring from the embers deep inside the holocaust, the only words she knew exploded from her lips. "I want you!" she cried, and the flames consumed her.

Brad's thrusting fingers slowed. His wicked tongue turned tender, stroking her lightly, smoothing the jagged edges of her climax. He pressed a soft kiss to the curls of her mound, and pressed his cheek to the cradle of her hips.

His warm, moist breath skittered across her skin, raising goose bumps. Cam managed to lift one limp, languid hand to stroke his hair. With herculean effort, she opened her eyes, blinking at the ceiling above her bed, not daring to look anywhere else.

"I didn't...I wasn't expecting..." Brad whispered in a rasp. "I don't have anything with me," he concluded in a rush of breath.

It took a full thirty seconds for his meaning to sink into her befuddled brain. When it did, she mustered a soft, "Oh."

Frank grunted. "Too bad. Go on home and jerk off, buddy. I'll stay here with Cam."

Silence ebbed and flowed around them. Her gaze traveled over the slope of Brad's back. His lanky legs were folded under him on the narrow bed. The waistband of his jeans gaped, giving her a tantalizing view of his firm, hard ass. His arms bracketed her hips, his torso was plastered to her thighs, and he kept his face averted, supplicating himself to her as he tried to catch his breath.

She raised her chin, staring at Frank defiantly as she said, "I'm on the pill."

"Oh, hell no!" Frank exploded.

"Camellia." Her name was both a plea and a prayer as it drifted from Brad's lips.

Frank moved to the side of the bed, glowering at her. "You don't know where this guy's been!"

"I haven't been with anyone in over four years," she said, holding Frank's gaze as her fingers trailed across Brad's shoulder.

"I can call and wake my doctor up, he'll tell you I'm healthy," Brad offered, jerking her attention from Frank when he raised his head.

Hope shone in his earnest green eyes, and she tugged at his arms, urging him closer.

"Aw, come on, he'd say anything to fuck you!" Frank cried.

Cam ignored Frank's outburst, focusing solely on Brad's eyes as he ranged his body over hers. The muscles in his arms stood in sharp relief as he held himself above her, waiting for her decision.

"I'm healthy," Brad said softly. "The healthiest I've ever been."

Brad's short bark of laughter startled her. Time seemed to stand still. A full minute may have ticked past as she tried to puzzle out the meaning of his last statement.

When she didn't answer him, Brad started to pull away. "I should go home."

"There you go, Einstein," Frank sneered. "Get out!"

Cam cut her eyes in his direction and caught the smug smile on Frank's face as he crossed his muscled arms over his chest. She hung onto Brad's wrists. His sensuous, sculpted lips flattened into a thin line as he stared back at her.

"Stay," she whispered.

"Aw, shit, Cam! You can't be serious!" Frank exploded.

Cam released her hold on Brad's wrists. Her fingers skimmed over his ribs, enjoying the ripple of his abs as she brushed over his stomach. She found the elastic peeking from the open waist of his jeans and slipped her fingers beneath the snug band. His body jerked and she smiled, basking in the heat of his gaze.

"I want you to stay." She stared past his shoulder at the ceiling and whispered, "I want you."

Quick as a flash, Brad was off the bed. The popping of buttons caught her attention. She watched as Brad shucked the remainder of his clothing.

They stood side by side—one dark, brooding, and angry; the other a golden flame dancing in the glow of the light. Rid of his jeans and shorts, Brad stood tall, proud, and clearly excited. The long, lithe lines of his body were a sharp contrast to Frank's pumped up bulk. Brad's body looked as if it were carved from marble. Frank stood still—an unyielding wall of hard, cold granite.

When Brad stretched out over her on the too-tiny bed, she welcomed his warmth. She cast a triumphant glance at Frank, and nipped at Brad's jaw. He parted her legs with his; the tip of his cock twitched at her entrance.

"So, I take it you decided to stay?" she whispered.

Brad gave her a breathless chuckle, but it was Frank who answered.

"Let me go, Cam," he growled, biting off each word.

Cam caressed Brad's stubbled cheek in her palm. Peering into his eyes she whispered, "Turn out the light."

With a muffled grunt, Brad reached for the switch. Darkness enveloped them as he cradled her head between his arms, tenderly smoothing her hair back from her brow. "Better?"

She nodded, blinking until her eyes adjusted to the dim light filtering in from the hall. She reached up, weaving her fingers between his. Brad's closed around hers tightly as he sank into her with a groan.

"My middle name is Eugene," he confessed in rush. Then, all of the words which eluded Cam tumbled from Brad's lips.

Chapter Thirteen

Every moan, every sigh, and each ragged gasp bounced off the walls. Frank tried to block it all out, but the rhythmic squeak of the bedsprings wouldn't let him. They called to him, luring him in, grating on his last nerve.

The bastard rasped her name in a voice so drenched in pleasure it almost made Frank's balls ache. She cried out, high-pitched and keening. "Cam," Frank groaned in response.

Black sludge roiled inside of him, dark and seething, its viscosity laced with jealousy and resentment. The sludge filled him, rising bilious and toxic in his throat when she called *his* name–the pansy-assed, college-boy, asshole who was fucking her in *their* room.

My room.

The squeals from the mattress slowed. The sound of labored breathing permeated the thick air. Their hearts were pounding, beating like war drums in Frank's ears. He forced the ooze threatening to choke him down into his stomach. He tried in vain to pinpoint the beat of Cam's heart.

Why would she choose him? Why would she do this here? Is she just doing it to torment me, or does she really want this guy? Why would she want him?

The guy talked a good game, Frank would give him that much. The words flowed from the slick bastard's lips like 10W-40. Not that a squeaky-clean, never-done-a-hard-days-work-in-his-life college boy would know what 10W-40 is... *He* used better words, and a lot of them.

Gorgeous, beautiful, and incandescent... What the fuck is incandescent supposed to mean? She's not a goddamn light bulb.

Oh, but he'd lit her up like one. Frank wanted to believe the pink flush of her skin was for him, but *Brad* had been the one kissing her, touching her, loving her.

Who the hell fucks a guy named Brad, anyway?

They whispered low and soft. Frank wanted to muzzle them both. He didn't want another peep out of either of them. Cam laughed, and the repercussions vibrated through the hole in his chest. She sounded happy.

This is Hell. This must be Hell.

The bed creaked as they shifted. He caught Brad's low chuckle rumbling deep and satisfied, muffled by the rustle of the bedclothes.

Cam sighed contentedly.

"I'm too long," Brad murmured when his foot banged against the footboard.

Frank snorted. "You wish."

Not that he'd looked. Okay, he may have peeked, but it wasn't like he had a choice—the guy was standing buck naked right next to him. He didn't want to look, but the shithead was naked in *his* room.

The seething ooze inside of him simmered. Pressing his hand to his twisting stomach, he tried to think clearly. Or, at least, think like a woman.

If he tamped down on the green monster breathing fire inside of him, Frank might admit—in a purely not-gay sort of way—that the guy was probably attractive to women. He was tall, but scrawny. Like he was the gangly kid who never grew into his arms and legs, or the 98-pound weakling who got sand kicked in his face in the back of comic books.

The guy obviously didn't lift weights. Hell, he probably doesn't lift anything heavier than a pen.

His mind flashed to an image of Cam's fingers tracing the muscles in the guy's back.

Well, yeah, everyone's got 'em. They just don't work them. He's probably one of those schmucks who pay a thousand dollars a month to go to some namby-pamby gym so he can aerobicize with chicks dressed like Olivia Newton-John.

His hand closed into a fist, unconsciously flexing the bulging muscle of his bicep.

Brad's not the type of guy who pumps iron.

Instead of making him feel better, the thought caught him short.

Maybe Cam doesn't want the kind of guy who pumps iron. She's too good for a guy with grease under his nails and grime ground into his pores.

He unclenched his fist and stared at the traces of black rimming his nails, embedded into his knuckles for all eternity.

She deserves better.

Cam laughed again, and the soft, sleepy resonance tore at him. The black goo bubbled and sputtered inside of him, working to a boil again. He wanted in on the joke. He wanted to make her laugh. He wanted to be the guy wrapped around her, holding her naked body close to his, burying his nose in her hair, and drifting off to sleep with the taste of her on his lips.

Brad murmured her name, and she sighed.

Frank closed his eyes and pictured her lips, swollen and deep pink, roughed from another man's kisses.

The sheet whispered against her. Skin chafed against skin, and Frank gritted his teeth. The lucky jerk was still touching her, stroking her. Cam's breathing grew deep and even.

"Camellia," Brad whispered. "My beautiful flower."

"Precious," Frank corrected automatically. "Precious flower."

Minutes crept by before Cam sighed in her sleep and murmured, "Frank."

For a moment the world stood still, silent and waiting. The whisper of the sheet stopped, and the chafing of skin on skin ceased. The mattress groaned. Brad's knuckles rapped against the headboard and he blew out a long, gusty breath. "Who the hell is Frank?" he whispered to the darkened room.

For the first time that night, Frank smiled. "Welcome to Hell, *buddy.*"

Chapter Fourteen

A damn bird tweeted outside the window—the stupid creature determined to grab the worm, because the sky wasn't even light yet. Brad should know. He'd been waiting for the sun for hours.

Cam slept—a still, silent and replete sleep beside of him. He should have been doing the same thing but found himself incapable of more than the lightest doze as the hours crept past.

Frank.

The name rankled, nettling his throat and piercing his heart like barbed wire. She said the wrong name. She should have been whispering *his* name as she drifted into sleep. Anger and frustration mixed inside him, combining with a hefty dollop of hurt, confusion, and wounded pride into a potent cocktail of...futility.

There was nothing he could do about it, and he knew it too damn well. He hadn't been able to pry himself from her side. Another man's name tumbled from the lips he'd been kissing, but he stayed super-glued to her bed, unable to let go.

He should go. The fact that he stayed here, listening to the sound of her breathing and waiting for her to say the name again was the sort of self-inflicted torture he would have mocked any other guy for tolerating. Brad knew he should wrest the control he'd given up from her graceful little hands and go.

He'd done it before, probably too many times. He was usually fairly skilled at extracting himself from a woman's bed, murmuring easy promises to call. Sometimes he meant what he said, others he didn't. Cam shouldn't be any different from the others. He shouldn't be so invested in her. He wanted to think he could walk away, but he couldn't seem to make his legs move.

The bird chirped and another answered.

Great, he brought friends, he thought sourly.

Brad stared at the ceiling and sighed in resignation. He gave his stomach an absent scratch and tried to breathe shallow breaths. Sex hung heavy in the air, thick and cloying, nearly choking him.

He'd passed the long hours of the night parsing every moment he'd spent with Cam in his head. One by one he picked through the murmurs, whispers, and moans— searching for a clue and coming up empty. He tried not to think about the sex. The sex made his mind fuzzy. He needed to be clear-headed now.

He was balancing on a tightrope, walking the edge of a cliff, hanging from a cable attached to a city skyscraper. Those were not things he did, as a rule. No one knew better than he what it meant for him to risk his heart. After all, he'd spent a lifetime guarding that vital organ vigilantly.

Cam mumbled in her sleep and rolled toward him. He turned to meet her. Soft, slow wisps of air tickled his chest, stirring the hairs and shooting shivers down his spine. He turned his head and peered through the crack in the blinds. The sky lightened to a pearly gray. The birds sassed him, singing songs of I-told-you-so. Faint streaks of pink reached through the darkness.

Cautiously, focused on moving one muscle at a time, he tested his mettle by easing away from her. Like a shadow he slipped from her bed. The blinds let in just enough light for him to prowl the room, gathering his clothes. Clutching them to his chest, he tiptoed to the door and padded into the bathroom.

Several splashes of cold water doused the urge to slip away without a word. By the time he wrestled his arms into his tee shirt, he'd decided that if he wouldn't wake her, he'd at least leave a note.

When he met his own gaze in the mirror above the sink, he wasn't surprised by what he saw. One thing he knew was the devastating toll heart trouble took on a person.

Long ago, his father's trembling hand closed around his, and he'd touched it. He heard it in the too cautious teasing of his sisters' voices and the faint aroma of fear that clung to him each time his mother hugged him. He'd noticed it in the pasty gray of Jim Stafford's skin and urged the older man to go to the doctor. He'd kissed Camellia Stafford, and now the taste of it lingered on his lips.

He ran his hand over his face and turned away from his reflection, and steeled himself to steal away.

Brad padded down the hall and back into her room. The quiet beauty of her face in the pink dawn light nearly broke him. He wanted to strip off his clothes and climb back into the bed with her, holding her close to his faltering heart. The gnawing need in his belly clamored to crawl into her and pound away until she screamed *his* name over and over again.

He spotted the nightstand and shuffled across the floor. He opened it with two fingers, exhaling with relief when he spied a thick spiral-bound notebook like he used to use in school. A quick look at Cam assured him his movements didn't disturb her sleep. He opened the notebook to a blank page at the back, and clicked the pen as quietly as possible.

The tip of the pen stood poised, its ballpoint pressing into the lined page. Brad stood frozen, unsure of what to say.

Cam snuffled softly, smacking her lips and burrowing into the pillow. Her fingers searched the empty space, seeking him out. "Brad," she mumbled, and his battered heart began to pound.

She clutched the edge of the pillow where he'd laid his head, inhaled deeply, and drifted back to sleep.

His teeth plunged into his lip, tamping the urge to answer her. His fingers twitched, and his hand began to move across the page. Light, deft strokes moved the pen with absolute certainty. Minutes later, he placed the notebook and pen on the nightstand, brushed her hair back from her face, and stole from the room without a sound.

Brad slipped through the front door, turning the lock on the handle before pulling it shut. The birds chirped behind him, probably calling him a pathetic loser, a wuss, or worse, a bird-brain. He didn't care. Whistling softly through his teeth, he headed for home feeling oddly energized.

****

"For God's sake, Susan, let the boy run. It won't kill him!"

He chuckled at the memory. His father had a way with words, even if his mother didn't appreciate his ways. Brad ran through the early morning quiet. Heavy footfalls cushioned by well-worn sneakers ate up the pavement with long, loping strides.

He turned his questions about this mysterious Frank guy over in his mind as he plodded through the still-sleeping streets. Cam said it had been four years since she'd been with anyone—if she was telling the truth.

She must be. Why else would she say that? Four is a random number. If she wanted to make something up, wouldn't she just say it had been a while?

He couldn't say it had been that long for him, but he didn't say someone else's name minutes after making love. If four years had passed, then this Frank guy must be long gone. But Cam obviously hadn't let go of him. Yet.

His first impulse was to ask the blunt question. He hated beating around the bush. He'd rather just put his cards on the table, find out what he's up against, and deal with it. But something niggled at his senses. A chilling tingle raised the hairs on the back of his neck, telling him there might be a reason he *shouldn't* ask about Frank.

Cam never even hinted at the existence of someone else. True, the hours they spent together were admittedly few, but usually he excelled at picking up the nuance of things people didn't say. He'd honed that skill at a young age.

"He doesn't have asthma," the doctor said regretfully.

Brad may have only been four or five at the time, but the tone of the doctor's voice told enough. Whatever he said, Brad's mother didn't want to hear. Since then, he hadn't needed an inhaler to make everything clear to him.

He rounded a corner and kicked it up a notch. Beads of sweat trickled down his neck, melding together into tiny rivulets, bumping along his vertebrae and soaking the back of his shirt. He loved the sensation of perspiration running freely down his spine. Sweat meant he was moving. He relished the dewy drops that flowed over him, painting him in bold, vibrant hues and coloring him alive.

For too many years he'd lived a line drawing of a life. Now he wanted to pull a Pollack on the world.

The moment he'd gone off to college, he'd ripped off the cotton-wool his mother wrapped him in as a child and set fire to it. The results of his declared independence were tear-soaked phone calls from his mother, pleading messages from his sisters, and an inkling of grudging respect from his father.

He pounded the pavement, but his thoughts remained jumbled—like pieces of concrete cracked and displaced by insistent tree roots. They scattered around

in his head, breaking apart but held together by gravity
and the earth beneath his feet.

He didn't blame Cam for loving someone before.
They haven't known each other long, they didn't know
each other well, and in the end, she had no reason to
believe they were meant to be together. Why would she
believe? Everyone she'd ever loved before is gone.
Including Frank, whoever he was.

No, he didn't blame her or anyone for doing what
they had to do to survive. His mother had done what any
good mother would do when forced to live with the
reality that her beloved child might die. His sisters,
though sympathetic to his constraints, often acted out of
a keen sense of self-preservation spawned by years of
living in a soap bubble.

He drank huge draughts of oxygen, and turned the
corner for home, shifting into a lower gear.

The perspective age and distance granted made
things a bit more understandable. Still determined to live
his life as he wanted, Brad grew more respectful of his
mother's worry. Once in a blue moon, he allowed his
sisters to hover over him like surrogate mother hens.
The helicopter routine made them happy.

As he grew older, Brad sympathized more with his
father. He understood the disillusionment his father
must have endured when, after waiting more than a
dozen years for a son, he ended up with a boy incapable
of handling a game of catch without getting winded. The
weight of his father's disappointment no longer threatened to crush him, he'd dashed out of the way just in
time.

He kept his gaze fixed on the sidewalk in front of
him as he passed the Stafford house, consoling himself
with the notion that if he gave Cam a little time and
space, she would grow to love him. Maybe not in the
way she loved her Frank, but perhaps in a new and

different way. Something they both would learn to live with.

He approached his driveway, but his feet didn't seem to want to heed the call of shower and work. Ten feet beyond the drive, he picked up the pace again, telling himself he'd take just one last lap around the block. One more lap, and he'd have sweated out the last vestiges of anger and humiliation. Once more around, and he'd be able to stand anything.

Everyone did what they needed to do to survive, and, for Brad, running proved he was alive.

Chapter Fifteen

Cam surfaced to streaming sunshine and the sweet trill of birdsong. She curled her fingers into the pillowcase, and tried to open her eyes but found her eyelashes had tangled and matted, clinging to each other in the thickest of webs. Her arms and legs would hardly move, as if she was swimming through Jell-O. Miniature marshmallows stuffed her head, making it difficult to think clearly.

The weight of the sheet was almost unbearable. Wrung-out, damp cotton clung to the bare skin of her back. She caught a whiff of Brad's aftershave mingling with the musky scent of masculine sweat, and hummed appreciatively. Cam pressed her nose into the pillow and took another hit.

"Sex hangover," she mumbled into the rumpled pillowcase.

The acknowledgement woke her slumberous limbs. She rolled over, pressed the heels of her hands to her eyes, and scrubbed away the last traces of sleep. Then she realized she was alone.

"Hello?"

Her call echoed through the empty house, and everything came back to her in a rush. Brad at her door, barefoot and irresistible. A tidal wave of heat flooded her cheeks as she recalled how her hands rushed all over him—eager, searching, grasping, and groping. The warmth abandoned her face, coursing through her body when she closed her eyes and remembered the long shadow of Brad's body falling over hers.

She opened them again, and the bright sunlight assaulted her with memories of Frank's sneering taunts, his obvious arousal, and her own wanton abandon as she surrendered to them both.

An icy spike of indignation caught her just under her breastbone, and the heat receded. Pressing her hand to the afflicted area, she swung her legs from the bed. Fury melted into humiliation before her feet touched the floor. She gaped in disbelief at the dress crumpled on the floor.

"Oh my God."

A flash of blind rage had her groping for the nightstand, searching for a pen or her phone, unsure which man she should skewer first. Something clattered to the floor, capturing her attention. She watched her pen roll under the bed and looked up to find her notebook open on the nightstand.

Cam sucked in a breath. "Oh no." She snatched the pad from the table, and clutched it to her chest. "What? Am I Bridget-Fucking-Jones now?"

Cam squeezed her eyes shut for a moment, blinking several times, trying to get a grip on the anxiety setting her teeth on edge. Cautiously, she let the notebook fall away from her breasts. She bit her lip and lowered her gaze to the page.

"Unh."

The involuntary little grunt freed her lip from captivity. Her heart swelled, hammering so hard she was sure it would burst from her chest. An ember of desire sputtered to life, tempering the pounding of her heart with a warm rush of pleasure.

The sketch was just ballpoint pen on lined paper, but the page came to life with each fluid stroke. Her hair was a matted mess, yet on the page wispy, delicate tendrils clung to the curve of her jaw and spilled into the hollow of her throat.

Brad thought her profile was a delicate cameo. Cam blinked away a veil of tears misting her eyes, and wondered if her eyelashes actually were a thick, feathery fringe. Pressing her fingers to her mouth, she had to defer to his expertise on the sensuous curve of her lips. After all, he'd kissed them over and over again.

The precise block letters at the bottom of the page were a bit of a shock. At first glance, their bold lines seemed too sharp a contrast to the tender rendering above. On second reading, though, she could imagine his deep, husky voice saying 'Now you see why I couldn't wake you.'

Cam held the book to her breast and searched the nightstand for her phone. A puzzled frown furrowed her brow. A full minute passed before Cam remembered she left it in her mother's office the night before.

She streaked across the hall and scrambled through crumpled sheets of yellow legal paper and scattered pens and pencils one handed. When she unearthed her cell, a foolish grin lit her face the moment she saw she had a text waiting. She retrieved the message, blushing like a school girl when she read: 'Good morning. You still owe me a date.'

Sunlight streamed through the window, warming the delicious ache of long unused muscles. Still hugging the notebook, she tapped her reply with her thumb. "Yes, I do," she murmured, pressing 'send.'

A minute later another message appeared. 'In a mtg. NOT where I want 2B. I'll call.'

Cam turned from the desk, a smug smile tugging at her lips as she sashayed to her bedroom. She paused at the threshold and cocked her head, studying the room critically. Her gaze strayed to the wall lamp then to the notebook tucked in the crook of her arm.

This is not where I want to be, she realized with stunning clarity.

Energized, Cam ripped the drawing from the spiral binding and closed the cover. After carefully placing the sheet of paper atop the rumpled covers, she opened the nightstand drawer and dumped the notebook. She spied the pen hiding under the bed and tossed it into the drawer before slamming it shut.

Thirty minutes later, she was showered and dressed, and throwing her rumpled clothing into the suitcase open on the floor. She gathered the file folder she had found in her mother's office, the legal pad covered in her increasingly messy scrawl, and dropped them into her luggage. Cam straightened the sheets and the faded rose-covered comforter.

She dropped to her knees and slipped the drawing Brad had given her into the folder her mother had left behind. The zipper whizzed through the stillness surrounding her. She yanked the suitcase onto its wheels as she stood, straightening her spine while she stared at the wall sconce defiantly.

"I wanted you, but you said I couldn't have you. You have no right to play games with me or him, or to hate me for wanting someone else," she said in a taut whisper.

Cam cleared her throat, determined to inject a little steel into her words. "This isn't what I wanted. I just wanted to come home to you, but if this is how things are going to be with us…" She jerked the handle of the suitcase, extending its length. "If this is how it *has* to be, then this is not where I *want* to be."

Chapter Sixteen

Cam let up on the accelerator and pressed the phone to her ear. "Hi. It's me."

"Hello," Brad answered.

Cam tensed when she heard his cool greeting and chewed the inside of her cheek. "Bad time?"

"This is fine."

"Good meeting?" she asked, wincing at the breathless tone of her voice.

"Unending."

Slightly daunted by his single word answers she offered a cautious, "I'm sorry."

Silence stretched between them for a moment. Brad drew a deep breath.

"Have dinner with me tonight? I need something to look forward to," he said at last.

"Tonight?" She glanced at the rearview mirror, trying to buy time to think.

"I plan on seeing you whether we include a meal or not, so we might as well have one."

A nervous laugh escaped her lips. "Oh, you do, huh?"

"Yep."

"Cocky bastard," she chided.

"I like to think of it as determination."

Cam slowed, checking the traffic in the next lane as she approached her turn off. A Honda's horn blared behind her as she edged her way into the line of cars waiting to exit. "Well, you are the pitch man."

"Where are you?"

"Almost home."

"Oh. Where did you go?"

She frowned as the lane slowed to a crawl. "Go?"

"You said you were almost home."

Cam laughed when she caught on to his confusion. "No, my home. I'm on my way back into the city."

"The city?"

She chuckled at his befuddled tone. "Yes. I live in the city, remember?"

"Right."

Her eyes narrowed at the grim note in his voice. "Is that a deal breaker? Am I not getting a meal out of this now?"

Brad had the good grace to laugh at himself. "No. Not at all. I just… I liked the idea of you being close."

"And readily available for your pleasure?" she teased. She was gratified when he groaned.

"Don't say that. I have a meeting with the board of directors for a chain of nursing homes in twenty minutes, and I can't walk in there, uh, distracted."

She giggled. Cam couldn't believe she honest-to-God giggled like a teenage girl. Trying to reclaim a smidgen of dignity, she shifted the phone to her other ear and coasted onto the ramp.

"Yes, I've heard those nursing home people are real sharks. You'll want to be on your toes." She waited a beat before dropping her voice into a deliberately seductive tone. "You have a suit coat, don't you?"

"Cruel woman."

She picked up the creak of leather and pictured him shifting in his chair.

"I've been thinking about you all morning," he murmured, matching her pitch.

Cam reveled in the shiver of anticipation rippling through her.

"Hard to be excited about pimping Shady Acres—which is not shady and the only acreage they have is a parking lot, by the way—but I get extremely excited when I think about you."

"And hard?"

"Do you doubt it?"

The drawing he'd left behind flashed in her mind. "Come to my place tonight? I'll cook dinner for you." The nervous tap of a pen abusing a desk, clicked in her ear.

"Can you cook?" he asked.

"Yes, I can cook. I also have a big bed. You might actually fit."

"When?"

The urgency in his voice erased all memory of his cool greeting. "Just come over after work."

Cam rattled off her address as she merged onto the surface street. When he repeated the information back, she scowled at the run-down storefronts littering her neighborhood.

"You might want to leave your car at the office and take a cab," she suggested.

"A cab? Why?"

"Because a sexy car like yours might be a little too much temptation for this neighborhood. Plus, parking sucks around here."

"It's not that bad, is it?" he asked, worry evident in his voice.

"No, but not great, either. Don't worry. I'll protect you."

"Very funny. I could pick you up and take you home with me," he offered.

Cam hesitated for only a moment. She heard the hope in his voice, but couldn't give in to it. "I need to be back in my own place."

Her statement was met with silence. She gnawed the inside of her cheek waiting for him to say something. "You still there?"

His voice was dull and flat when he answered, "I'm rushing you."

"No, you're not." A crackle of static broke the nothingness that hummed between them for a moment.

"Please tell me you drove the Buick," Brad grumbled at last.

Cam snorted. "I can't park that boat here. Come over at about six?"

"Looking forward to it."

"Me too."

She ended the call and hooked a sharp right, heading for the neighborhood supermarket and praying the suspicious rattle her car was making was nothing serious. The last thing she wanted to do was prove him right this early in the relationship.

****

When he conquered the last flight of stairs looking every inch the dapper advertising executive, she was waiting at the door. His pearl gray suit garnered only a sweeping glance. Cam reached out, snagged him by his bright red tie, and pulled him close.

She molded her body to his, tipped her chin up, and whispered, "Well, hello, Don Draper. Are you here to pull my hair, ravish me, and leave me for dead?"

He covered her mouth with a hard, fast kiss. "I should. Only bad girls send text messages like that to a guy trapped in a room full of gerontologists."

She laughed, letting the tie slip through her fingers as she turned and led him into her apartment. "I couldn't resist."

He caught her at the kitchen door, wrapping one arm around her waist and burying his nose in her hair. "Something smells incredible."

"Hmm. Could it be me or dinner?"

"Both."

"Mm hmm. Dinner is almost ready," she said, gently removing his arm from her waist. She saw the unmasked ambivalence in his grass-green eyes and laughed. Moving into the tiny galley kitchen, she grabbed a pair of oven mitts. "Later. I have beer in the fridge."

"Trying to distract me," he grumbled.

Beer bottles clinked, and she opened the oven door. A thick silence filled the room.

"Stop looking at my butt," she ordered.

"No."

Cam shot him a wicked glare and extracted a roasting pan from the oven. She sensed him scooting closer as she kicked the oven door closed. When she looked up, he took a deep appreciative sniff.

"Meatloaf? You made meatloaf?" he asked, a faint rasp roughing his voice.

Her stomach dropped. "You don't like meatloaf?" When he continued to gape at the pan she quickly said, "We can go out. Or order in, if you want."

He stole a glance at her, his eyes darkening. "You *are* trying to seduce me."

Cam couldn't help but smile. "Working?"

"Am I drooling? 'Cause that would be embarrassing," he added. The bottles he held clanked together when he wrapped his arms around her and pulled her flush against his chest. "I promised myself I wouldn't propose until the second date."

"Yeah, best to try to play it cool," she whispered, stroking the silken tie cinched at his neck before slipping one finger under the knot and working the tail loose.

****

"Note to self: Meatloaf drives Brad wild," she murmured, brushing a soft kiss to his bare shoulder, soothing away the bite mark she'd made a short time before.

He chuckled as her hair slid through his fingers, fanning across his bare chest. "*You* drive me wild. The meatloaf was just a bonus."

She sprawled across the bed, half draped over him, her legs tangled with the endless length of his. The crinkling hairs on his leg tickled the arch of her foot as she stroked his calf. "What makes guys all nutty about meatloaf? My dad would almost do a happy dance when I made it for him."

Brad smiled, trailing one fingertip along the line of her jaw, tipping her chin until their eyes met. "Meatloaf means home."

"Home?"

"Comfort food. Meatloaf is made by someone who cares enough to squish their hands in hamburger, peel potatoes and carrots, and seal it all with a delicious ketchup kiss."

She chuckled and pressed her face into the curve of his neck. "Boys are so easy."

"Not easy. Not all meatloaf is created equal. You can order some in a restaurant, but it isn't the same."

"It isn't?" she whispered, fascinated by his theory. "Is this the Tao of Meatloaf?"

"I haven't had meatloaf since my parents moved to Arizona."

She toyed with the crisp hairs on his chest. "Have you missed, uh, meatloaf?"

"Sometimes," he conceded with a wry smile.

Cam circled one flat, brown nipple. She smiled against his throat when his skin beaded against the pad of her finger.

Brad's hand closed over hers, his long fingers curling her palm as he carried her hand to his lips. He kissed the fingertip that teased him then nipped it with his teeth. "Be careful," he warned.

"I don't wanna." Cam propped herself on her elbow and stared at him, using the same finger to outline his lips. "I don't want to be careful."

She was rewarded with a gusty laugh. "I think we're a little past being careful."

"What's that supposed to mean?"

One broad shoulder twitched in a shrug. He reached up, twisting his fingers into her tangled hair once more. "I've never... You're the first woman I've ever been with like this."

"You were a virgin?" she gasped, her eyes widening.

Brad rolled his eyes. "You weren't very gentle with me," he joked.

Another laugh caught in her chest, then burst free— unleashed by the heady realization that she had never laughed this much with any other guy.

"I'm sorry," she said, trying for solemn but landing somewhere just short of giddy.

He wrapped his arms around her, pulling her onto him. His green eyes shone warm with delight. Cam gasped when his fingers bit into her hips, pressing her to the hard length of his erection.

"Insatiable," she murmured.

"Infatuated," he whispered. His hands moved to her buttocks, squeezing her flesh insistently. Brad teased the crevice of her ass with the tips of his fingers as he ground against her. "You have the most incredible ass," he growled.

"Too big."

He closed his eyes, his hips arching into her as her damp folds slid the length of him. "It's a wet dream," he retorted, punctuating his statement with a laugh that morphed into a groan.

A tiny thrill shivered through her. "It is?"

"Mmhmm."

The muscles in his arms flexed, and he lifted her. His fingers burrowed into the soft flesh of her ass as he nudged against her damp folds. His eyes locked on hers, seeking her approval. She sank onto him, enveloping him. He groaned long and low in his throat.

He pulsed deep inside of her. "I've thought about you hundreds of times," he confessed in a rush. "Dreamed of you."

"Brad…"

Brad jackknifed off of the bed, propelling her back until she straddled him. His lips found her neck, peppering her skin with soft, sucking kisses. "Never like this— bare…" He groaned again, and she began to move. "They lie."

"Who?"

"The Trojan people."

"Trojan people?" she asked, unable to grasp his meaning.

"They lie, they lie," he chanted. The vibration of his voice rippled across her skin, raising goosebumps. "Nothing feels as good as being inside you. Christ, Cam, you're incredible."

She moaned, finally catching his drift. "So I *am* your first in a way."

"Only," he grunted.

"Me too," she whispered, letting her head fall back. "Tell me how it feels."

"Hot. Wet…" His hands slid up her back. He cupped her neck and shoulders, impaling her on his slick shaft. "Strong…animal…"

Her surge of pleasure proved his words right. She was fluid and light, buoyed by the arousal soaking them both. Cam gripped his shoulders, pushing him back on the bed, smiling as he acquiesced, but claimed her ass again as a consolation prize.

"Primal?" she suggested, circling her hips enticingly.

"Yeah, primal, whatever."

She leaned forward, rising on her knees until he almost slipped from her heat, letting the curtain of her hair brush his chest. "Tell me what you want to do with me."

The fire in his eyes flared, golden flames danced in their green depths. His voice was thick with gravel when he asked, "You really want to know?"

"Oh yeah, I really want to know," she purred.

Reluctantly releasing his hold on her buttocks, he slipped his hands under her hair, gathering the waves in his palms. A few tendrils slipped through his fingers as he cradled the back of her head, holding her gaze.

"I want to love you slow and sweet," he began in a whisper. Cam blinked slowly, humming her approval. Without warning his hips surged off of the bed and he plunged into her. "I want to fuck you until you scream," he rasped. He gripped her hips, and thrust hard and fast as he pulled her down on him.

A strangled cry ripped from her chest and he answered with a groan.

"I'm gonna do it all, Cam," he promised, his eyes blazing with desire. He rolled up, his abs bunching under her hands, trapping them between their bodies. "I don't care what kind of animal it makes me, I need you every way I can have you."

The muscles in her thighs burned, but it was nothing compared to the sweep of heat making her blood simmer.

"I love being inside you...bare inside you...just me and you. I want to fill you up... I want you so full of me you'll never think of anyone else, dream of anyone else."

His breath was hot and moist against her ear. Her nails furrowed the hard ridges of muscle bracketing his spine; his pressed into the crevice of her ass, spreading her wide as she rode him hard and fast.

"God, yes. Fuck me, Cam," he murmured against her throat.

His teeth abraded her windpipe. She raked the length of his back with her nails. A rush of pleasure gushed through her when he flinched. His tongue washed over the pulse throbbing under her jaw, and she moaned a low, desperate warning.

"Only me," he whispered as she careened toward the edge.

Cam clasped his head between her palms, forcing his face up. She kissed him hard and hot, pouring everything she had into him the moment his lips parted. He grunted his surrender, and she caught his moan with her mouth.

"Come with me," she whispered, bracing her hands on his shoulders and arching her back as the waves of sensation carried her away. "Come with me..." she chanted, riding him with abandon, pulling him over the edge with her.

Chapter Seventeen

Well, if it isn't my old friend, darkness. Frank sighed. *Nothing like having your consciousness hijacked by Simon and Garfunkel's greatest hits.*

His lips curved into a sneering smile as the pity party began in earnest. Logically, he knew he passed weeks and months cloaked in darkness before, but the inky blackness never seemed this acute.

Without Jim Stafford's daily routine to mark time, days and nights melded together into nothingness. For years, he welcomed each day with the drip of the coffeemaker. Evenings were once heralded by the jingle of keys in the door and the soothing sounds of Cam's father shuffling between the freezer and the microwave.

Days had passed since Cam left, maybe even a week. Her parting words still rang fresh in his ears. No, it wasn't fair to intrude on her little interlude with Campus Ken, but life isn't fair. The idea of Cam letting some guy touch her hours after he'd touched her, or tried to touch her, made him shudder.

He didn't have to play fair. She didn't play fair either. He loved her, had loved her forever, and now he would forever see her naked and panting, staring into his eyes while another man held her. Now that was a picture planted in his brain.

Too bad they drowned out the sound of silence. He smirked, momentarily amused by his own play on words.

The moment ended and time stood still again. The darkness stretched unending, pulling him into a yawning abyss of self-pity. He counted seconds between cricket chirps, talked back to birds, and tried to drown his thoughts in the drone of distant lawn mowers. The counting proved better than attempting to figure out why he'd been trapped here.

Why?

Frank hadn't asked the question for so long, the thought startled him when it popped into his head. The more he thought about thinking about his predicament, the more he wondered why he hadn't bothered to think about why he was here. The answer was too easy: Cam.

Cam was the keeper of his fate. He had to believe she was the reason he's still here, and that she alone held the key to his prison. For the past ten years, he'd become more and more convinced her diaries were his ticket out.

She has to come back for them. She can't leave the house vacant and unattended. She'll have to come back and deal with the house and deal with me.

He just hoped she'd be back sooner rather than later. Sooner seemed bad enough in the oppressive silence that enveloped him. Later would be too many cricket chirps to count.

Chapter Eighteen

Brad was well aware they were living in a bubble. A fragile bubble—shiny and bright, colored with opalescent swirls of lust, comfort, and wonder. They didn't float to the surface until Sunday, when he insisted he needed to go home.

After an intense round of bargaining, he convinced her to stay at his house that evening with the understanding he'd gather enough clothing to last the week at her place. They'd been inseparable since he took his first bite of meatloaf.

Cam's moods made being with her a delicate balancing act, but one Brad quickly grasped. He realized she was in mourning, and although she wanted him near, she also didn't want to be smothered. For his part, the last thing in the world he ever wanted was to be the man who held her down.

When he'd appear at her door in the evenings to find her moody or perturbed, he'd change into shorts and a tee shirt, pull on his running shoes, and pummel the grimy city sidewalks until he could control his disappointment. Whatever misgivings he might have about the breakneck speed of their relationship would be lost the moment he folded her into his arms, holding her close as she turned loose the worries of the day.

Until he broached the subject of her father's house, Brad hadn't grasped the level of her ambivalence.

"Do you know what you want to do with the house?" he asked one night.

Cam smiled, but the rising corners of her mouth didn't chase the dull pain from her eyes. She ducked her head and began to kiss her way down his chest. "I know what I want to do right now."

He couldn't suppress his half-amused, half-aroused chuckle as she trailed her tongue along the center of his stomach. "What's that?"

She nuzzled the curls that sprung up at the base of his cock.

His body stirred. He held himself still as every muscle in his body seemed to stretch and thicken. "Cam."

"Only one thing I want," she whispered.

Hot, moist breath teased his pubic hair. Pinpoints of awareness prickled his skin, allowing every semblance of lucidity and reason to trickle from his pores. Still, he felt compelled to make a last ditch effort. "We need to talk."

Cam's velvet lips closed around the tip of his dick, and a prolonged groan pronounced him a goner. She stared at him as she pulled away, her blue eyes heavy-lidded with power and arousal. Her lips quirked into a tiny smile when their eyes met.

"Can't talk now; my mouth is full."

Brad's laugh turned into a groan. He fought the urge to thrust into the plush, wet welcome of her mouth. Brad fisted the sheet, yanking one corner free from the mattress. Cam pressed her hand to his hip, pinning him to the bed with her gentle caress. Her lips shone red and moist. He licked his, torn between claiming hers with his mouth and pushing her head between his legs.

"What did you want to talk about?" she asked innocently.

"What?"

Cam's answering smile was full and slow. "That's what I thought."

His hands plunged into the tangled mass of her hair. His hips twitched with barely suppressed need. She moaned her approval and pressed a sweet kiss to the velvet tip of him. Cam closed her lips around his stiff shaft, his hard skin gliding over her tongue, plunging toward the sweet, silken pull of her throat.

His fingers knotted in her hair, tugging at the roots. "This what you want, Cam?" he panted. Her distracted hum ignited a flame of anger in his belly. "You don't wanna talk, right?"

She moaned, and the vibration almost set him off. Her fingernails dug into his hips, piercing his skin; he surged off the bed and into her mouth. "Isn't this what you wanted? You don't want to talk, your mouth's full now, right, Cam?"

She responded with an ardent tug and he was trapped—helpless against the onslaught of arousal and emotion she stirred in him. Cam hummed again and the sensation pinned him to the bed. Desperate, he clawed for what little control he had left and pushed her away.

"Hey!"

"Don't play games with me, Cam," he panted. "You don't want to talk, you tell me you don't want to talk and why, but don't try to fuck with my head."

Anger flashed in her eyes. "How about I don't fuck you at all?"

Brad pulled his hands from her hair, holding them up in surrender. "That's your choice, but you don't get to use me, Cam."

"Use you? You're the one camped out in my apartment eating my food and hogging my remote!"

He propped his weight on his elbows, and stared into her eyes. "I'm crazy about you. You don't have to distract me with sex. Just be honest with me."

"I said I didn't want to talk about it."

"And then you did what you had to do to keep *me* from talking about it." When she didn't say anything, he sighed. "I want more than this." He gestured to his crotch and softened his words with a small smile. "I'll give you anything you want, Cam, but don't try to handle me."

The belligerence faded from her gaze, but her jaw tensed. "I don't want to talk about that," she said flatly. "It hurts."

"Fair enough." His lungs shuddered as he drew in a breath. "As long as you realize I'll probably keep prodding you." The corner of his mouth turned up when he glanced at his still-aroused body. "I love prodding you."

She rolled her eyes, and he collapsed on the bed, folding his hands placidly over his stomach. "Gonna finish what you started?"

Cam snorted, her gaze raking his body. "I don't know…" He could see she was still tempted, despite her temper. "Gonna be nice if I do?"

He laced his fingers behind his head, leaving himself completely vulnerable. "I'll be exactly what you want me to be."

"Bastard," she whispered, lowering her head again.

He closed his eyes, trying to ignore the rush of adrenaline leftover from the confrontation. Brad concentrated on each urgent pull of her mouth, the downy softness of her lips and tongue, and the sweet heat of her surrounding him. She worked him slow and steady, letting the tension build again.

He opened his eyes to find her watching him through her lashes. "So beautiful," he whispered, barely aware the words escaped his lips.

Cam shifted, pulling away from him with a soft pop.

"No," he groaned. His entire body tensed, keening the loss.

"Yes," she countered, crawling over him like a sleek, golden cat.

Her tongue swept into his mouth dragging him under. She captured his tongue, drawing him into her mouth and sucking gently while she disentangled their bodies. She broke the kiss and claimed the last shred of his pride when she pulled away.

"I'll beg."

She smiled. "Begging would be nice, but unnecessary."

The next thing he knew, she'd swung her knee over his head, reversing her position and granting him a tantalizing view of her damp, pink folds. "Let's both get what we want," she murmured, lowering herself to his mouth as she bent and took him in hers.

Within minutes, they lay damp, panting, and spent. Cam sprawled across his chest and torso, her cheek pressed into his thigh and her knees bent against the headboard.

When he managed enough breath to speak, he said, "I'm going home this weekend. I have grass to cut, a house that may have blown up, and milk spoiling in my fridge." He ran his hand along the back of her thigh then pressed a kiss to her calf. "Cam?"

"Okay," she mumbled against his thigh.

"I want you to come with me."

She sighed, the rise and fall of her breast teasing his semi-aroused flesh. He gripped the backs of her thighs, kneading the taut muscle up to the rounded mounds of her ass. "As much as I love the view, I wish you would look at me."

Cam pushed up and drew her knees toward her chest, flipping her mane of hair back as she sat up.

He steadied her, tracing the sinuous shape of her back with his fingertips. "I'll admit it's purely selfish on my part. I don't want to miss you."

She turned, eying him speculatively. "Would you?"

"Maybe a little," he drawled.

A hint of a smile teased her lips. She climbed off of him and knelt on the bed beside him, searching his face for the answer she needed. "A little?"

Brad rose from the bed, his face centimeters from hers. Brad tucked her hair behind her ear and gave her a crooked smile. "I might pine."

"Will there be keening, wailing, and the gnashing of teeth?"

He sensed her capitulation, and fixed her with a solemn stare. "If left to my own devices, I may spend the whole time drawing naked pictures of you."

She cocked her head. "Don't you do that anyway?"

"Not when I'm with you."

Cam sighed and turned away, staring at the darkness beyond her bedroom window. "I know I need to go. I just left everything," she admitted in a whisper.

Brad pressed his forehead to hers and stroked her tangled hair. "That's okay. We'll just go to my place. Everything else is yours to take or leave."

Cam nodded, moving his head too. "Along with the strip mall."

"We can extort free footlongs from the sub shop."

"We'll stay at your place?" she asked cautiously.

"Yep. I'll even let you use the whirlpool tub."

"With bubbles?"

"With me," he replied firmly.

****

Over the next two days, Cam warmed to the idea of gathering a few things from her parents' house. Proud he didn't have to prod any further, Brad picked up a bundle of moving boxes from a storage place, a roll of bubble wrap, and some heavy duty tape before swinging by her apartment Friday evening.

They stopped in a neighboring suburb for dinner, lingering over the meal, and using the cover of the dimly lit room to devour each other with their eyes.

She circled the rim of her wine glass with the tip of her finger and shook her head. "You're so smug."

"You're breathtaking."

"I'm a mess. I need a haircut," she replied, running a self-conscious hand over her head. "I'm all scraggly and grown out—like the camellias in Dad's yard." Her smile was forced when she reached for his hand, tangling her fingers in his. "Do me a favor?"

"You can have all the favors you want, particularly if they come with the words 'do me' attached," he said with a laugh.

"Funny boy," she chided. "Seriously, would you do something for me?"

"Anything." Cam grinned at his automatic response, and he flushed. "I need to learn to play hard to get," he grumbled.

"No, I like you easy." Her fingertips slid against his, the rasp of her skin sparking an entirely different rush. "Would you trim back the camellias for me tomorrow? They're out of hand."

Brad's fingers tightened on hers. "No."

"No?"

"Nuh uh. They stay the way they are," he said gruffly.

Taken aback, she scowled at him. "What? Why?"

Brad gathered her delicate fingers in his palm and covered them with his other hand. "I asked your dad about them once, but he didn't want them cut back."

Cam looked shocked. "Why not?"

He pulled her hand to his lips, grazing her knuckles with his lips. "He said he liked them that way. Told me he never knew how to take care of them, so he liked to let them grow wild and free. Like you."

"Me?"

He nodded, turning her hand over in his to expose her palm. He placed a soft kiss to the tender skin and closed her fingers around the imprint of his lips, hoping she'd hold onto the tender caress, praying he could be enough for her. "Just like you," he murmured, staring into her eyes.

Cam wet her lips, her gaze dropping to their hands. "Do me another favor?"

"If I can," he qualified.

"Take me home with you," she whispered.

Chapter Nineteen

Cam stood in the center of the living room surrounded by half-packed boxes and holding a frog figurine. The glazed ceramic was cool and smooth, but the frog's painted face was alive with barely contained mirth. For days she'd been turning this project over in her mind, trying to come to grips with the prospect of dismantling the only house she'd ever called home.

She knew packing her parents' belongings would make her sad, but finding forgotten treasures like this little frog made her happy. Realizing she'd never live here again was one thing, but actually beginning the process had almost proved too daunting. When Brad mentioned needing to spend some time at his place in order to get things done around the house, she realized she couldn't put this off any longer.

Cam glanced at the array of boxes at her feet, a frown wrinkling her brow when she tried to remember which carton held the objects she intended to take home right away.

Thankfully, Marjorie Crutcher had taken care of returning the plethora of casserole dishes and pie plates she'd abandoned in the kitchen when she fled. She'd also volunteered to help Cam box the items she wanted to donate to local charities. All Cam had to do was focus on the items she wanted to keep—things like this gaudy little frog.

She jumped when Brad walked in. He wiped the sweat from his face with his discarded shirt then he narrowed his gaze at the multitude of cartons.

A guilty smile curved her lips as she cooed, "There's my eye candy."

"Water," he panted, heading for the kitchen.

Cam wrinkled her nose at the half-packed boxes and followed him. "I know this is a mess, but I have a system."

Brad filled a glass from the tap and chugged the cool liquid in three long gulps. "A system for systematically destroying the rainforest with your cardboard box fetish?"

She balanced the figurine on her palm, holding the frog up for him. "Leonard Leapsalot."

His eyes warmed, and he struggled to hang on to his stern scowl. "Leonard, huh? I remember his story."

"Well, now you've met him live and in person," she answered pertly. She placed the frog on the counter then turned to look him in the eye. "I want to ask you to do something for me."

One inquiring eyebrow rose. "I can't lose the shorts. There are little kids running through the sprinkler across the street," he explained, gesturing to the front door.

"Damn," she whispered, shooting him a flirty glance. Cam propped her hip against the counter, and met his gaze. "No, seriously..."

Brad frowned into his empty glass. "Sure. Anything."

Cam inched a little closer. "I love it when you say that." She took a deep breath. "I've been working on something for the past couple of weeks—"

"The *Kama Sutra*? Yes, I know."

"And you've enjoyed every moment," she retorted. When he didn't bother trying to deny his complicity, she plunged ahead. "A story. I've been working on a story."

"The mating habits of septuagenarians?"

"*Crawdad Cove*."

Brad gave her a puzzled frown. "The mating habits of crawdads?"

Cam shook her head, frustration and embarrassment warring in her stomach. "A story. Fiction," she clarified.

Brad set the glass aside and leaned back against the sink. "Fiction? I thought you didn't write fiction."

"I don't... I mean, I haven't," she said in a rush. "I am now."

"You are?"

She turned to the bright green ceramic frog. His face held such hope, his smile such promise. No wonder her mother had found the little guy so irresistible. Cam felt the same tug each time she wrote about Peter Pincer.

"I found an idea in one of my mom's files, and well, I thought I'd try."

Brad nodded and braced his hands on the counter as he prompted, "And?"

A slow smile crept across her face. "I like it," she whispered. She could feel the heat of his stare and dared a peek from under her lashes. "I'm writing the story of this kid—well, a crawdad kid—Peter Pincer, who's destined from birth to protect the Crawdad King, but he has a weak pincer. His parents try to hide the disability from everyone, afraid they'll be ostracized...." She trailed off, giving him a sheepish smile. "It may not be any good."

"I bet it is."

"You might be biased," she said with a laugh.

"A little, but I'm still betting on you."

A rush of pleasure warmed her cheeks. "I was wondering if you'd—and you totally don't have to," she said, lifting a cautionary hand. "Would you...."

"Yes, I want to read it."

A relieved laugh sputtered from her lips. "Okay. Well, that wasn't what I was going to ask, but I guess you'd have to."

"What were you going to ask?"

She gazed up at him, her eyes searching the mossy depths of his. "If you like the story would you, uh, draw it?"

"Draw?"

"Like you did for *Greystone Manor*."

"You want to make your book into a comic book?"

"I thought 'graphic novel' was the hip term," she teased, shooting him a nervous smile.

"Are you serious?"

Cam began to second guess herself. She shook her head and took a quick step back. "Nah, forget it, stupid idea."

"No, it's not," Brad said, pushing away from the counter. His lips curved into a wide boyish grin. "I'd love to."

"You would?"

"Hell yeah. It's been forever since I've drawn anything for fun." His hands closed around her arms, his fingertips slipping into the sleeves of her shirt. "Tell me about it."

Cam smiled, bracing her hands on his chest. "Later. You still have two more lawns to cut."

"Wow, Cam, this is big," he said gruffly.

"Not big. Small. Tiny. We may be the only two people who ever read it."

Something flickered in the deep forest green of his eyes. "I hope not."

"You think?" she asked, uncertain.

"Let's do it."

Her fingers trailed over his sweat-slicked skin, stroking the coppery hairs curling in the center of his chest. "You're always all for doing it."

Brad laughed. "Did you really think I'd get enough after only two weeks?"

"I wondered."

She *had* wondered if the intensity would wear off. She wondered if what they had could possibly be for real. For the past two weeks, they'd spent every free moment together and some not-so-free moments too. Even those were nice—sitting on the couch tapping away on her laptop while he sat at the opposite end doing the same thing.

She was afraid this rush wouldn't last. She feared something would happen and they couldn't make their relationship work. Things were too good. That made her nervous. They were too good together, and the thought terrified her.

He dipped his head and kissed her tenderly. "I don't think I'll ever get enough of you," he whispered.

Despite her nerves, she felt hope unfurling in her chest, opening like the velvety petals of a flower. "Promise?"

"Cross my heart."

She smiled and drew a tiny 'X' over his heart before she pressed her lips to the damp curls on his chest. When she pulled away, she spotted the faint white line hidden by the hair between his pecs.

"I keep forgetting to ask. What happened here? Bar fight?" she asked, tracing the thin scar with her fingernail.

"Broken heart," he answered, sounding mildly amused.

"Who was she? I'll kill her," she grumbled. Looking up at him, a sly smile slid across her face. "Or send her a thank you note."

He glanced at his chest then met her gaze levelly. "I had a hole in my heart."

"A hole?" she repeated, shaking her head in confusion.

"Ventricular Septal Defect." His voice was cool and flat, devoid of any emotion. "I was probably born with the hole, but they didn't figure it out until I was about five. I was sick all the time when I was little. They thought I had asthma."

"Whoa."

Terror, icy and slick, rained like sleet on her heart, coating the delicate petals of blooming hope and crushing them under its weight.

He nodded. "Every time I had a growth spurt, I'd get worse. I had one surgery when I was five, but it didn't close all the way, so I had another at eight."

"Oh, wow," she whispered, tracing the straight line of the scar.

She closed her eyes and saw herself rushing through the emergency room doors, heard her father's friend's mumbled words of consolation, picking out the only words that mattered: coronary, cardiac arrest.

"I couldn't do much as a kid. I'd have a hard time breathing or faint. My mom would freak out."

After a beat, Cam realized he was waiting for her to say something. "I bet she would," she managed at last.

He nodded. "I drew a lot."

Overheard snippets, echoes of distant and not-so-distant past haunted her.

Massive heart attack—he just fell out of his chair, Cam.

It was an aortic aneurism. She just collapsed in the produce section of the A&P, poor thing.

"I see," she whispered, distracted.

He crooked one finger under her chin, urging her to meet his gaze. Cam tried to blink back the tears filming her eyes. "I'm fine, Cam. Healthy and whole," he reassured her.

"Yeah, I know," she murmured, swiping at the tears clinging to her eyelashes. She tried to force her lungs to function. "That had to be so hard, though."

Brad shrugged. "Harder on my folks, I think. For me, that's just the way things were."

A sudden surge of indignant horror gripped her. "You run! You run every day!" she blurted.

"Okay, you missed the healthy and whole part," he said grimly.

"Stop saying hole!" Cam snapped. "Running is hard on your heart!"

"That's whole with a *W*, and running is good for my heart," he argued. She opened her mouth to retort, but his eyes flashed green and glassy, hardening before her very eyes. "Don't, Cam. Don't think like that. I can't live my life thinking those thoughts."

Cam planted both hands on his chest and pushed away from him. A tiny stab of pain pierced her own heart when he let her go. "How do you know what I think?"

"I can see it in your eyes, Cam. You're staring at me the way they all used to stare at me. 'Don't do that, Bradley, that's too hard for you. You don't want to play basketball, Bradley. Here, draw me a pretty picture.' That's what you want to say, isn't it?" he demanded, his voice hard and bitter.

"Brad—"

"I won't. I won't live a half-life anymore, no matter how much my family loves me, no matter what anyone says. I stopped a dozen years ago, and I won't go back. I can't."

"What about what the doctors say?"

"The doctors say I'm fine!" he exploded, throwing his arms open wide. "I'm fine. I'm fucking perfect, but no one wants to hear that, do they?"

Cam gaped at him, stunned by the vehemence that shattered his usually calm demeanor. His hands clamped around her arms, anger and frustration seeping from his pores and radiating from him like sweat. Her heart fisted in her throat. Her pulse drummed in her ears, but the cadence was off—too slow, too mournful.

"Do you love me?" he demanded.

She opened her mouth, her mind screaming the word blocked by the pebbles of fear clogging her throat.

When she didn't answer, Brad visibly deflated. "Maybe it's too soon," he mumbled.

He released her and drew the back of one hand across his mouth, squeezing his eyes shut. Her heart ached. "Brad... "

When he met her gaze, his eyes were a deep, mossy green, clouded with worry. "The problem is, this isn't too soon for me, Cam," he said quietly. "I love you. I'm *in* love with you."

"That scares me," she whispered.

He took a step back, nodding slowly. "Me loving you, or letting yourself love me back?"

"Both."

"Okay." He took a breath and nodded again. Brad straightened his shoulders. "Well, my heart is whole, Cam. In one piece and strong." He met her gaze levelly. "Yours, if you want it. It's up to you."

He scooped his shirt from the counter. Cam watched as he shrugged into the damp cotton, desperately searching for the words she wanted to say, but they wouldn't come.

"I've got two more yards to do," he said, reaching for the back door.

"Brad."

He twisted the locks and jerked the door free of the warped wooden frame. He pushed through the screen door with such force the handle slammed against the house, jolting her from her moorings. When she reached the door, he was jogging down the steps.

Brad paused at the bottom and stared back at her, his jaw clenched and his hands curled into fists, but his face remained impassive. "I'll finish up, and then I might go for a run. You know where to find me," he told her, then disappeared around the side of the house.

Cam pressed her hands to the wire mesh. Her nails scraped against the screen, clawing for purchase on the slippery slope she was tumbling down.

"Don't leave," she whispered, but he didn't hear her.

She stood frozen at the screen door. She could tell him she already loved him, but she wouldn't. She may not be able to help falling for him, but everyone she'd ever dared to love left her, and she'd be damned if she'd make leaving easier for him.

She pulled her cell from her pocket and dialed. It was cowardly to call, she knew that, but she didn't have an ounce of bravery to spare. She also knew he'd left his cell on the kitchen counter at his house. When his voicemail kicked in, she took a bracing breath and waited for the beep.

"Hi. Listen, I think I'll stay here. Maybe we've just had too much quality time together," she said with a bitter laugh. "I'll, uh, I have the Buick. We can talk in a day or two. So, um, bye," she finished lamely. Cam ended the call and switched the phone off.

She stomped back to the living room, planting her hands on her hips and glaring at the nearest box. Words bubbled in her throat. They might be flimsy and fragile, but their importance choked her.

She dealt the box a swift kick, wincing as a heart-stopping crunch echoed in the room. Tears pricked her eyes and she stumbled back, jerking in an awkward dance while shards of broken glass tinkled to the bottom of the carton.

Cam rushed down the hall to her mother's office and tore the dust cover from the pristine typewriter. The machine purred beneath her trembling hands as she wound a sheet of yellowed paper between the rollers.

Cam dropped into the chair, her fingers poised over the keys. Closing her eyes, she swallowed her tears and willed the words to flow instead.

The typeball twirled and whirled, spinning faintly inked letters onto the page. She struck the key for a period and sat back trying to absorb the line she'd written.

'The screen door slammed, his sudden departure knocking her back like a bullet piercing her heart.'

Cam sat on the edge of the seat, settling her fingertips on the keys once more. Tentatively, she began to peck out letters again. She closed her eyes and typed by touch. On the page, she chased after him. Each keystroke indelibly inked her love for him on thin onion skin paper. She let her fingers speak for the ache in her chest and write the love story she was too afraid to let herself live.

Chapter Twenty

Frank listened to her moving around the living room and dining room. Newspaper crumpled and the occasional bursts of air being squeezed from thin plastic compartments ripped through the last vestiges of silence. The soft rasp of carefully wrapped memories being packed into cardboard boxes combined with Cam's mindless humming soothed him. For the first time in weeks, Frank was completely at ease. Then, the front door closed.

His cheeks burned hot the second he caught the guy's voice. *Brad*. Brad was back. Brad was still around. Frank clenched his teeth. A strained muscle twitched and jumped in his jaw as he eavesdropped on their conversation.

"Comic books? You *are* the 98 pound weakling, *Brad*," he muttered. A minute later, his attitude toward the guy softened a bit when he recognized the mix of awe and pride in Brad's voice. "Yeah, she is amazing, and don't you forget it." Frank whispered.

He continued to eavesdrop on their conversation, stiffening when Brad said, 'a hole in my heart.' His hand strayed automatically to the worn Metallica shirt he wore. With the tip of his finger he pressed the fabric into the tiny hole at the center of his chest.

Then all hell broke loose. Cam was scared and upset. Brad didn't handle things well, his voice rising in frustration as he tried to hold firm against her arguments. If Frank didn't hate him so much, he might have admired the jerk a little bit. You have to have balls to stand up to Cam—he should know.

Then, the guy pulled a one-eighty and poured his Swiss cheese heart into Cam's tiny, ruthless hands, practically begging her to love him back. Frank groaned and shook his head. "Aw, come on. You just handed her your balls."

The screen door slammed. Cam made a phone call, and cut the poor bastard off at the knees.

He wasn't shocked when she kicked the box. Cam always did have a temper that flared and burnt out like a match. The footsteps coming down the hall didn't surprise him either. Frank's muscles tensed, bracing for the confrontation he knew had to come. He was determined to handle it better than poor, old Brad. He waited for her, but she never came.

Instead, she holed up in the room across the hall. A low steady hum rumbled in the still air. He frowned, trying to place the noise in his memory. A soft 'ding' signaled a memory and recognition began to dawn.

He actually cringed when she cranked a piece of paper into rollers. The click of her nails on the typewriter's keys only served as a faint precursor to the clack of the letters striking the page. She picked up speed, pummeling the keyboard.

The air crackled with energy, but Frank couldn't find the handle on what was happening. Power swirled through the house, wild and free. Emotion dipped and shifted like the wind—billowing through the curtains, beating against the walls, and whipping the air in each room into a frenzy. The walls pulsed, alive with promise, and shimmering with vitality. It nearly scared the afterlife right out of him.

Frank bit the inside of his cheek. For the first time in years, he was dying to know what she wrote.

****

Hours later, the house creaked under the weight of silence. Cam was still here. He could hear her breathing.

He tasted the flavor of her heartbeat in his throat. The desk chair creaked as she rose, ripping another page from the roller.

Her footsteps were slow and plodding, rising and falling heavily, as if each step pained her. She stumbled across the floor of her room. Frank's relief was palpable when the bedsprings crunched and coiled under her weight.

Cam sat still, unspeaking and barely breathing. He tried to use the force of his will to make her turn the light on, but her mind was elsewhere. Pages whispered and rustled against one another, keeping her secrets. He closed his eyes, desperately trying to envision the words on the paper crinkling in her grasp.

Slowly, the crisp sheets caved in. Frank scowled, listening to them crumple. For a second, he couldn't grasp what she was doing. Then everything came clear to him in a rush.

The sound of her hands wadding her spent emotion into a ball punched him in the gut. The squeeze of her fingers muffling on the words that had flowed out of her clawed at the edges of the dark hole in his chest. The thwack of the ball hitting the wall struck him. The dull thunk of the bundle falling to the floor nearly brought him to his knees.

"Cam, turn on the light," he growled into the darkness.

She drew in oxygen through her nose, and exhaled in a whoosh.

"Cam." His voice broke on the plea.

The mattress squeaked. Her fingernails tapped against the metal base of the sconce, and with the soft snick of the switch he was free. He stood on the rug beside her bed and planted his feet in a wide stance, his hands clenched into fists and tucked under his arms. When he looked at her, he almost reeled back.

Cam sat on the edge of the bed, her blue eyes calm and impassive, her delicate fingers curled into her palms, her sensuous, mobile mouth set in a thin line. She stared straight through him at the wall—stoic, silent, and stone-faced.

Frank lunged at her, grasping her by the shoulders and giving her a rough shake. "Damn it, Cam."

Her head lolled like a rag doll, but when her eyes met his, her lips quirked into her familiar half-smile. "Hello, Frank."

His hands fell to his sides, and the fight drained from him. "Hi, Cam," he croaked.

When her gaze drifted past him to the wall the snub hit him full force. "What the hell are you doing?"

Cam blinked and cocked her head, looking at him with a bewildered expression. "I'm wondering if I should strip the wallpaper in here and repaint."

"What?"

"Brad says you only need to update the kitchen and the baths, but Brad says a lot of things..." she murmured, craning her neck to inspect the far corners of the room.

Unable to stop himself, Frank muttered, "He said he loves you."

Cam gave him a distracted nod. "Heard that, huh?" She gnawed her lip. "I think I will paint. Beige or khaki. White trim, or some other nice, neutral color."

"Dammit, Cam!"

She jerked as his explosion struck her. Cam quickly schooled her features and inquired politely, "Okay, what color do you want?"

Frank fell to his knees in front of her and grabbed her arms, forcing her to look at him as shimmering sparks of white light shot from his fingertips.

"Do you love him?" His voice came out hoarse and rough as he searched the dull blue of her eyes, demanding an answer.

"Doesn't matter," she answered in a flat voice.

"Yes, it does!"

The tip of her pink tongue touched her lip, wetting the spot she had bitten. "No. It doesn't."

"So that's it? The guy tells you he was a sick kid, and you dump him?" he asked, incredulous.

"He has a hole in his heart!"

"*Had!* Had, Cam, *had!*"

He released her, his mouth working, but no further sound came out. She turned her bland gaze on him, and he exploded.

"You wanna see a hole in your heart? This is a hole in your heart!" he roared, jerking his Metallica shirt up to reveal the tiny hole left behind by the bullet that stopped his heart.

Cam stared at the tiny black hole for a moment then raised her eyes to his. "I'm not going to let him leave me," she said stiffly. "Best to let him go now. It won't hurt so much now." Her voice broke on the last word.

Frank dropped the hem of his shirt. "Do you really think so? Do you think he would leave you? The guy's crazy about you. Even *I* get that!"

Cam's voice rang as soft and bleak as a death knell. "He may not want to, but he would."

"Are you nuts?"

"They all leave!" she shouted. "Everybody I love leaves, and I'm stuck here alone!"

"You've never been alone! You don't know what alone is!"

She stared at him for a moment then inclined her head slightly. "You're right. I've never been alone. I've always had you."

Cam reached the nightstand drawer, shooting him a scornful look. "I can let Brad go, can't I? I don't need him…I have you," she said, pulling her notebook from the drawer.

She placed the journal on the comforter beside her within his reach and trailed her fingertip along the coiled wire that bound it together. "You're not always very easy to get along with, and we'll have to figure something out about the sex thing, but I'll always have you."

"I'm not real," he whispered, his gaze locked on the notebook.

She pressed her hand flat on the cover, spreading her fingers wide. "You are to me. Maybe someday, if we can stop fighting long enough, we'll be able to make it work."

"This won't ever work." Frank ran his hand over his face. His fingers scraped against the twenty-year-old five o'clock shadow on his jaw.

"You don't love me, Cam," he whispered.

"What do you know?" she snapped.

"I know I don't make you laugh and hum and make those annoying, squeaky girly noises."

"I don't make squeaky girly noises."

"I don't make you worry and fret and turn yourself inside out because you're so scared you can't see straight," he insisted. "You've never been scared of me."

She reached out to touch his cheek. "I don't need to be. You're safe. You're here."

Frank pressed his lips together, leveling her with a steady gaze as he waved a hand at the crumpled ball of paper on the floor. "If I open those pages, I'm going to read all about how much you love him, aren't I?"

"No!" Cam lunged from the bed, knocking him over in her haste to get to them first.

Electricity zapped through the room, jolting their tangled limbs, flashing brightly around them as they grappled for the wad of paper. Frank's fingers closed around the ball and his palm sank through to the floor boards.

With a triumphant laugh, Cam snatched it from the floor, cradling the ball in both hands and pressing it to her chest. "You can't have it. It's mine," she panted.

She crawled to the bed and grabbed the notebook. "They're mine, not yours. My memories, my hopes, my dreams," she whispered. "That's why you can't have them."

Incensed by her taunting tone, Frank made a grab for the notebook.

"It's not right," he grunted, growling in frustration when his fingers slipped right through the cover, landing on the soft curve of her breast.

"No?" Cam looked at him, raising a sardonic eyebrow when he didn't pull his hand away.

She opened her arms, the notebook clutched in one hand, the crushed ball of paper in the other. They both stared at his hand covering her breast.

Motor oil that would never be washed away darkened his fingernails, and coarse black hairs bristled on his knuckles, sweeping up the back of his hand. His fingers looked so incongruous against the pearly pink of her shirt he wanted to cringe. Instead, they curled into the rounded mound and he raised his head to meet her gaze.

Her mouth twitched, and a sad smile lifted one corner of her lips. "I guess where there's a will there's a way, right, Frank?"

Drawn into the depths of her fathomless blue eyes, he leaned in. His eyelids grew too heavy to hold open and his lips met hers in the barest of kisses. He opened his eyes. Cam waited for him—stoic, silent, and stone-faced, just like his mother.

Pain ripped through his body, tensing every muscle and setting each nerve ending on fire. Her breath tickled his lips, and he pressed his mouth to hers, desperate for more. He parted her lips with his tongue. A burst of rage fueled by her passivity nearly quenched his pain.

Beneath his fingertips, he felt the dull thud of her heart for the first time. His tongue touched hers and the salty tang of her tears shocked him. He tasted her heartache. Her pain pulsed against his palm.

He kissed her again, and they burst into flames.

Frank wrenched himself away as Cam's eyes widened. For a split second, fire danced in her palms. She closed her fists and the flames died. Jerking them to her chest, the remnants of her journal and the ball of papers she held sprinkled to the floor in a shower of cold, gray ash.

Frank gaped at the traces of soot on the floor. Cam gulped in air, her eyes wild and searching as she tried to assimilate what had happened.

He reached down, trailing one finger through the mound of dust. His mouth tightened into a thin line as he eyed the ash of the pages that were moments before a testament to her love for another man.

"Maybe this is for the best," he mumbled.

Cam's eyes grew round as saucers, and her hand flew at his face. He jerked back on impact, but her fingers left no trail of sensation where they'd struck his skin. He felt nothing.

Cam hit the floor, collapsing before his eyes, folding into herself in tiny creases that cut too deep to ever smooth again. The tight coil of her body shuddered, wracked by the silent sobs too painful to voice.

Frank scrambled back, gaining his feet and staring at her in amazement. This was Cam, his Cam. His precious flower lay crushed at his feet.

"They were mine," she whispered.

She's broken. I broke her. I break everything I touch.

I never dreamed I could do this. Not Cam. She's indestructible.

"My dreams...mine."

Frank's fists clenched at his sides. Desperate to do something, he stooped and scooped her from the floor. Cam didn't fight, flail, or lash out at him. He almost wished she would. He placed her gently on the bed and gazed down at the crumpled ball that was the woman he loved.

He sat on the edge of the bed, giving her a moment to acknowledge or dismiss him. When she did neither, he stretched out behind her, curving his body around hers. Ice-blue light shimmered and shifted between them, dimming the golden glow of the lamp.

He stroked her hair, but the silken strands sifted through his fingers like air. He wrapped his arm around her and pressed his hand to her stomach, but couldn't pick up the beat of her heart. Frank buried his face in her hair, closing his eyes and thanking God he could no longer smell her sorrow or taste her heartbreak.

I touched her and now she's broken. I did it.

I swear I'll never touch her again... I just have to figure out how to fix her.

Chapter Twenty-One

Cam didn't stretch out against him, though the comforting bulk of his body braced hers. She didn't move. She didn't dare. Suddenly her body was light as a feather, as insubstantial as fog—drifting, floating away on air so thin she could hardly breathe.

The weight of Frank's arm kept her anchored, but she couldn't be thankful for the safety of its mooring. She wouldn't be comforted by the warmth of his fingers, or the stalwart glow of the energy flowing between them. As much as she wanted to be lulled by the gentle cadence of his voice as he fed her the tidbits of information she used to crave, any response she may have made melted on her tongue.

Staring blankly at the wall festooned with rosebuds, she let every word wash over her, knowing she'd never be able to grasp them. The words were too late. She lay numb and unfeeling while Frank slipped through her fingers like mist.

It didn't matter whether he'd thought his friend was going to buy hot auto parts and not drugs on the night he was shot. He wouldn't be around in the morning. The dark tales he told of his father beating his mother did nothing to stir her. She couldn't fight fate. Any response she may have made to the sweet words he murmured in her ear turned stale and bitter on her tongue.

She had nothing to say. Words weren't real. Frank wasn't real.

She registered the distant creak of the screen door opening. Frank tensed, his body growing taut and rigid behind her, but he didn't budge. Soft footfalls echoed in the hallway. A long shadow loomed in the doorframe, and Brad's voice wafted into the room.

"You left the back door wide open," he called to her, his tone edged with worry and impatience.

"No shit," Frank grumbled. "And you strolled right in, buddy."

"Cam? Are you okay?" Brad asked, moving cautiously into the room.

"Does she look okay, Einstein?" Frank retorted.

She would have laughed if she had the energy. Despite the ache in her heart, the byplay between the two men in her life tickled her, but her muscles were too weak to produce the sound.

Brad fell to his knees beside the bed, tenderly stroking her hair and ducking his head to gaze worriedly into her eyes. "I've been calling for hours," he whispered. "I told myself I wouldn't come chasing after you, but I can't help it."

"Pansy," Frank muttered. "You've got the guy completely whipped, Cam. Not that I'm any better."

Brad reached into the pocket of his shorts and extracted a folded sheet of paper. "Here, look." Brad unfolded the sheet and held up a sketch of a determined-looking crawfish colored in bright red pencil. "I'm not sure if he's supposed to be red, but I didn't think you'd want grayish-brown..."

The sheet of paper fluttered to the floor.

"Cam, I'm sorry," Brad said in a rush.

She stared at him blankly, trying to catch his drift, wondering if he was apologizing for the shading of the drawing or something more.

"All my life, I've had people telling me what I can't do. They used love as a weight to hold me down," he whispered. "And, because I loved them too, I let them."

He took a deep breath, his fingers sifting through her hair, his eyes fixed on hers. "I was their only boy. I'm eight years younger than Steph. A happy accident," he said with a bitter laugh. "Except I didn't turn out to be too happy for them."

"Another frickin' miracle baby," Frank grumbled.

Cam tensed and wet her lips. "My parents had given up. They were older, a lot older when they had me," she whispered.

"Then you know what it's like, that weight, the expectations..." Brad said gruffly. "I can't do it anymore. I grew up on the sidelines, safe and secure, watching everyone else live their lives and being too afraid to get into the game."

"Your dad only wanted you to be happy," Frank reminded her.

"When I was old enough, healthy enough, I broke free," Brad continued. He ran an agitated hand through his rumpled hair. "God, all I wanted to do was run, Cam. Run away from the doctors, and my mother, and the worry. I needed the wind in my face. I wanted to move, to sweat, to feel my heart pounding and prove that it wasn't going to stop."

"You never know that," Frank muttered.

Cam stiffened then stretched as far as she could, trying to push Frank away and needing to keep him close at the same time.

"I had to fight for it," Brad whispered. "Fight my own weakness, my mother's hysterical need to smother me, and the doubts my father never said out loud..."

His fingers stroked the curve of her cheekbone. "I had to fight my own fear to find a balance between what's safe and what I needed." He gave her a wry half-smile. "There's a reason I'm not a starving artist, painting what's in my heart, and wandering the streets of Paris."

A breathy laugh sputtered from her lungs, and Frank's arm contracted around her, banding her to him like steel.

"If I painted what's in my heart, France would be littered with pictures of you," Brad whispered and pressed a soft kiss to her forehead.

Frank's arm relaxed a little but remained in place.

"You asked me to cut back the camellias," Brad said gruffly. "I can't, Cam. They're everything I want to be, just like you were everything to your dad."

Tears burned behind her eyes and Cam blinked to battle them back.

"I know you miss him, and you're scared," he whispered. "It's okay to be scared, but I'm not okay with letting fear rule your life."

The tears began to flow, blazing trails along her cheek, and pooling hot and salty on her lips.

Brad brushed one away with the pad of his thumb and carried the tear to his lips. Her breath caught in her throat as he tasted her sorrow. A sob broke free when his mouth touched hers, drinking her pain. She kissed him back, drawing on his lips, filling her lungs with him.

"I love you, Camellia Rose Stafford," he whispered, stroking her hair as he pulled back to look into her eyes. "It's terrifying, the way my heart skips a beat whenever you're near me."

"But worth it," Frank whispered.

"You're worth the risk," Brad murmured, his voice soft but filled with conviction.

Lifting his arm from her waist, Frank placed his hand on her hip, pulling her gently toward the edge of the bed. "Let him in, Cam."

She shifted, making room for Brad on the narrow bed. He smiled and climbed onto the mattress, propping his head on his arm. His feet bumped the footboard, and his knees nudged her calves, but somehow they fit perfectly. She pressed her hand to his chest, absorbing the slow, steady strum of his heartbeat through her fingertips.

"He loves you. I love you. That's never going to change, not even when your heart stops beating," Frank assured her.

"I love you, too," she answered.

Cam closed her eyes and nestled into the curve of Brad's neck. Comforted by the throb of the pulse in his throat and the heat radiating from Frank's body, she heaved a gusty sigh. The two men she loved chuckled, the vibration of their bodies buffeting her while they held her close between them. As she drifted off to sleep, she inhaled deeply, drowning her fears in the heady aroma of Polo cologne mingling with fresh-cut grass.

Chapter Twenty-Two

Frank watched as Brad fought sleep. Brad's eyelids were barely at half-mast, but still he blinked each time a puff of Cam's breath hit his skin.

The guy was driving Frank nuts. Jealousy oozed inside of Frank, stirring with each lazy blink.

Cam shifted. Her round, soft bottom pressed against Frank's groin when she draped one long leg over Brad's.

A weird, sizzling sensation prickled the hairs on his arm, and Frank looked down to find Brad had draped his arm over Cam. Brad's flesh and bone sank straight through the muscle and sinew of Frank's own arm as if he wasn't there.

Frank yanked his arm away, running his hand over his forearm to soothe the itch that burned like fire. "If I were alive, I'd swear some kinky shit was about to go down here," he muttered.

Frank glared at Brad over the top of Cam's bowed head then rubbed his hand over his face. "God, I feel old. I was driving before you were born."

He rolled halfway onto his back, clinging to the edge of the mattress to keep from tumbling off and staring at the ceiling. Some strange need to connect with the guy in some way that didn't involve Cam made him ask the first thing that came to mind.

"What kind of car do you drive?"

When he got no response, Frank sighed, rubbing the worn fabric of his tee shirt over his stomach. "A sedan," he concluded, "but something with a little pep." Frank blinked and shifted away, sifting through his memory. "Are Beemers still hot? You look like a yuppie."

Cam snuffled in her sleep, inching closer to Brad.

Frank turned and saw her hand gliding over the guy's back. "Nuh uh, not again. Take that shit somewhere else. I'm not watching that again."

A contented sigh whispered through the air as Cam settled again. Brad exhaled slowly through his nose and Frank chuckled.

"Sorry, buddy. I know she's somethin', but I need you to resist for this one night." He whispered to the ceiling, "This one last night. After tonight she's all yours."

Minutes passed in silence. Frank drummed his fingers against his stomach. He dared a peek at Brad, only to find him still awake.

"Aw, for fuck's sake, would you snuggle up to her like the little kitten you are and go to sleep? I've got things I gotta tell her, and they're none of your goddamned business."

Brad blinked again.

Frank shifted onto his side, propping his head on his hand and glaring at the other man. "Okay, fine, I've got some things I can say to you, too."

Brad stroked one long tendril of her hair, smoothing the silky strands against the satin skin of her arm.

"Precious," Frank began. "She's a *precious* flower, not just a beautiful one, okay? You've gotta comfort her and take care of her, but you can't let her push you around. She's strong...resilient." He closed his eyes, searching for whatever advice he had to give. "She'll push you. She'll push you as far as you let her. Trust me on this one; I know."

Frank opened his eyes and stared hard at Brad. "Let her push you some. You'll be a better man for it, but don't let her go too far. You have to push back."

Brad's head bobbed a little as he closed his eyes.

"She's a coupe. A racer; sleek and fast. You can pamper her, keep her buffed and polished, but you can't be afraid to rev the engine a bit." Frank trailed one finger over the curve of Cam's shoulder, his voice growing deep and soft. "Turn her loose, and enjoy the ride."

His voice trailed away. Frank basked in the silence shrouding the still house. Crickets chirped outside the window, and he counted the seconds in time with their song. A soft snore rent the air, wrenching a laugh from deep inside of him.

He pressed his lips to Cam's hair, keeping his eyes open to catch the way the waves shimmered like old gold when he touched her.

"Your boyfriend snores," he whispered into the tangled waves. The rasp in his voice made his throat ache. "He snores, and you talk in your sleep. You're gonna make a hell of a couple."

Frank nuzzled her hair as he whispered, "If I was ten years younger … and alive, of course, *I'd* teach your boy here what it means to fight for something. *Someone*," he corrected. "I'd fight for you, Cam, if I could." He forced himself to roll away again. "But I can't," he said, his voice bleak and heavy with resignation.

With a grunt, he rolled up, sliding off of the bed to kneel alongside as Brad had a short time before. Cam moved, slipping her leg between Brad's, meshing their limbs like gears. They rolled slightly, claiming the sliver of space Frank had vacated.

"You fit," he whispered. "I'm not gonna make any piston jokes. I'm not gonna fight it, either. This is yours. Like a dream, you know? Once you've had a dream, no one can take it away."

He stood and gazed at their entwined bodies. "I won't be back," he warned gruffly. "You don't need me anymore, Cam. You won't remember me. I'm just a dream—a shadow of someone you thought you knew."

Skirting the end of the bed, he walked toward the light shining from the wall above her bed. His fingers closed around the switch. The worn grooves rubbed like raw silk against the whorls of his fingerprints.

"I wanna tell you I love you, and I'll be yours...well, forever. I'll be thinking about you, Camellia Rose, my precious flower, and dreaming of all the things we could have done together." Before he turned out the light he whispered, "Isn't that what dreams are about? Possibilities?"

Chapter Twenty-Three

Brad woke slowly, roused from sleep by a spate of incessant chirping. His growl of disapproval was met with a sleepy giggle. Cam snuggled closer, moving her head from his arm to his chest. When her hand slid from his chest over his stomach to linger at the button on his shorts, his body tensed and coiled, preparing to strike.

He covered her hand with his, stilling the playful index finger dipping into the waistband and teasing the ripple of elastic beneath. "Good morning," he croaked.

"You're finally awake."

"I am now." Brad released his hold on her hand and exhaled slowly giving himself over to the dawn patrol. "I hate those birds."

Cam chuckled, flipping the tab of his zipper up then leisurely pulling it down. "One advantage to living in the city—the only birds around are pigeons."

"I'm not sure that makes up for the foul bag lady sitting on the corner and screaming obscenities."

"Well, you *do* have a delicious ass," she purred, "and it *is* a shame to cover it up."

"Come here."

Cam tossed her hair over her shoulder and rolled on top of him. A slow, sensuous smile curved her lips and made his heart skitter. "Thanks for coming over," she whispered, pecking a soft kiss to his lips.

"Self-preservation. I was afraid I wouldn't be able to sleep without you yammering in my ear all night."

"I have to do something to drown out the snoring," she retorted.

Sunlight streamed through the slats of the blinds, infusing her hair with the glow of amber, goldenrod, and saffron. Brad wound one tangled lock around his index finger then tugged, urging her closer.

When her lips hovered millimeters from his, he whispered, "Let me try this again. Good morning. I love you."

Spiky fawn-colored lashes tipped in gold swept to her cheekbone. A tender pink blush rose high in her cheeks. Cam wet her lips and opened her eyes, meeting his gaze with eyes the color of a summer evening.

"I love you," she breathed.

"Do you?"

She nodded, the corner of her mouth twitching into a smile. "God help you."

He stroked the smooth skin of her jaw with his thumb, cupping her cheek. "I'll take whatever help I can get," he answered. "I'll probably screw up a lot."

Cam smiled and rewarded him with a long, lingering kiss. "Mmm, screwing what?" she murmured when she pulled away.

"No screwing." His hands slid under her shirt. Brad hummed with satisfaction when he found her smooth, supple skin.

"No?"

He pushed the shirt higher, letting the cotton bunch under her arms as he urged her up. "No, not now," he murmured, stripping the shirt over her head. His fingers found the clasp of her bra. She sighed as the elastic gave way. Offering her a crooked smile, he slid the straps over her shoulders. "Maybe later," he whispered, letting the scrap of lace and satin fall to the floor.

Wordlessly, they shed the rest of their clothes. Cam grasped his shoulders, her nails biting into muscle as she pulled him onto her. He blanketed her, sunlight striping their bodies while they stretched out together, skin against skin.

Her toes tickled his ankles. His tongue traced the shell of her ear. She shivered in his arms and set his flesh on fire. Their lips met again and again, seeking solace, giving reassurance, and keeping promises unspoken.

The lush comfort of her body cushioned him. Her hair smelled like strawberries and bananas. Her skin was as sweet as honey. He cupped her breasts in his hands, molding them to his palms as her nipples rose.

Cam pulled his hands away, lacing her fingers through his and pressing them high above her, nudging the headboard. Her hips circled in an earthy dance that spoke to his soul. Her skin slid over his like silk.

Every nerve ending in his body screamed her name. "Camellia," he breathed.

Her smile blossomed slowly, her eyes lighting with love and affection then darkening with desire as their bodies aligned. "Bradley."

"Brad," he corrected automatically.

"We've met...Eugene," she whispered, closing her eyes and wrapping her legs around him, opening for him.

"Funny girl."

He sighed, sinking into her wet heat slowly, savoring the feel of her body absorbing his. When he was sheathed in her, safe and warm in her slick embrace, he held himself still, lowering his head into the curve of her neck. Her pulse beat strong and steady beneath her delicate skin.

"I love you," she whispered, her fingers tightening on his.

He raised his head and she smiled. "Just practicing."

Brad nodded, returning her smile as he began to move slowly. "Keep at it," he said, hoarse with emotion.

Her heels pressed into the backs of his thighs. "I was going to say the same thing to you."

"I take it back. I want to love a girl who isn't a smart ass."

"Too late, you already love me," she answered smugly.

"Yeah. Yeah, I do." He lowered his lips to hers, drawing her bottom lip into his mouth. Her lips tasted warm and sweet, like berries ripened in the sun.

His eyes locked on hers as he drove her higher with every thrust of his body. He blinked, etching the image of her face in his brain. Every detail stood in sharp relief. Her lips parted, soft and slack in anticipation. The depths of her blue eyes clouded with pleasure.

She pressed her head into the pillow, arching her neck, exposing the slim ivory column of her throat. Unable to resist, he covered her pulse with his mouth, exulting in the tremor that rocked her body when his teeth scraped over her skin. Cam cried out. Spasms of release shuddered through her, squeezing him, pulling him deeper, and demanding everything he had to give.

Brad collapsed on top of her, burrowing into her neck, drinking in her scent. Cam wriggled her hands free from his, running them over his back and soothing his trembling muscles. A soft chuckle bubbled into a laugh as she hugged him close to her.

"Eugene," she giggled.

The sound of her delight ignited a spark of joy that burst inside of him like a firecracker. Brad pressed a smacking kiss to her ear. "Precious flower," he whispered before flopping onto his back.

Birdsong filled the air, buoyant tweets and chirps bouncing off the sun-streaked walls. "God, I love those birds," he confessed with a gusty sigh.

Cam rolled onto her side, curling into him, draping her leg over his. "I'm a little jealous."

His lips twitched into a smile. "Don't worry. It's only infatuation. I'll hate them again in a few minutes."

She stretched luxuriously, pressing her length sinuously against his. "Let's stay in bed all day."

"Excellent plan. The boxes will pack themselves."

"Eh, they're not going anywhere," she mumbled, trying to suppress a yawn and failing miserably. Rubbing the arch of her foot over his shin, she kissed his chest, a satisfied smile curving her lips when his nipple pebbled. "I had the strangest dreams last night."

"Hmm?" he hummed, distracted by the plump curve of her bottom.

"I dreamed I wrote a book."

Startled from his reverie, he gave her butt a playful pat. "Wow, from articles on how to pick up guys in the supermarket, to children's stories, to the great American novel in just a couple of weeks," he laughed. "You don't do anything halfway, do you?"

"Why bother?" she asked with a dismissive wave of her hand.

He laughed, hugging her tightly as she burrowed into his chest, plumping him like a pillow. He drew lazy patterns on her bare back, smiling as her muscles grew loose and lax and she melted into him.

Cam sighed contentedly and murmured, "Brad."

Maybe it was the seductive softness of her sigh, or perhaps something in her tone. Brad stiffened, incapable of biting back the question that nagged at him each night when they drifted off to sleep. Afraid to look at her, he stared at the ceiling, bracing himself for her answer even before he dared to ask.

"Cam? Who's Frank?"

Silence simmered in the air. "Frank?"

"Yeah."

"Frank? Where did you hear that name?" she asked, clearly befuddled.

"You talk in your sleep."

Cam raised her head, a crease of confusion bisecting her brows as she shook her head. "I don't know anyone named Frank."

"No?"

"Huh uh."

Brad stared into her guileless blue eyes, searching them for any trace of deception. "Okay," he breathed, exhaling at last.

She cocked her head, propping one arm on his chest. "Were you worried?"

He knew the chance to play it cool had long since passed him by, but male pride dictated he try anyway. "Not really," he answered with a shrug. "Just curious."

Cam stared at him, amusement dancing in her eyes. "Good. I'm glad you weren't worried."

They lapsed into silence for a moment.

"It made me crazy," he admitted in a rush.

Cam flashed a satisfied smile. "Good. I like you a little jealous." Cam sandwiched a centimeter of the thick morning air between her thumb and forefinger. "Not a lot, a little."

He gave her hair a playful tug, palmed the top of her head like a basketball, and pushed it back to his chest. "Tell me about your novel."

Cam snickered. "I don't remember what I was writing."

"I like thrillers and spy stories. Shoot for one of those."

"I think it was a romance."

His eyebrows shot up. "Oh yeah? One of the ones with the shirtless guy ripping the dress off the girl?"

"A bodice ripper?" She snorted. "How do you know about bodice rippers?"

"I have a mother and two sisters. They consume those things like candy."

"Uh huh," she answered in a tone laced with doubt.

"Hey, you're the one who's the expert on how to bag unsuspecting guys in auto parts stores."

With an indignant harrumph, Cam flicked her hair off of her shoulder. "Please... Too much work. I don't pick up guys in supermarkets or auto parts stores. I do it the easy way."

"Oh? How?"

Cam grinned as she sat up, deviling him with that elusive dimple and framing his face with both hands. She smoothed his hair over his ears, her eyes twinkling as she shrugged and said, "I seduce the gardener."

Chapter Twenty-Four

Cam no longer jumped each time she heard the jarring 'zzzzt-zzzzt' of Brad's drill. For the past two weeks, she'd spent her days alternating between packing her parents' belongings into a forest of cardboard boxes and tapping away on her laptop when procrastination sang its siren song. Every evening, Brad had stalked through the increasingly bare house making lists and mumbling 'kitchens and baths' under his breath each time she made a suggestion for another improvement.

The living room was depleted of knick-knacks and redecorated with boxes—packed, taped, and labeled in his neat block letters. The dining room suffered a similar fate. The china cabinet was vacant and stood sentry over a brigade of similarly marked boxes. Marjorie had made good on her promise, hauling boxes and bags of Cam's father's clothes and shoes off to various charities while Cam wept over a pair of monogrammed cufflinks she'd found in a dresser drawer.

In the front flowerbeds, dozens of daylilies sent shoots reaching for the sky. In Lily Stafford's office, only the desk and file cabinet remained untouched. The IBM Selectric was packed in its case and stored in Brad's spare bedroom. Her trusty laptop sat in its place. Her screensaver bounced, ever-ready to be reawakened the moment inspiration struck.

Cam dumped a handful of empty hangers into a box and closed the door to her bedroom closet, scanning the room for her next victim. Her gaze landed on the nightstand. She grabbed the flap of a cardboard carton and moved purposefully toward the unsuspecting bed table, intent on wreaking havoc.

"I hate packing!" she called when the whir of the drill died out.

"I'm not painting these cabinets," he answered.

Cam dropped onto her butt in front of the nightstand. "You love to paint!" The drill drowned out anything he might have mumbled in response.

She opened the drawer and scowled at the detritus scattered inside. With a groan, Cam reached for the wastepaper basket, dragging it across the floor to her. A handful of abandoned pen caps, forgotten sticks of gum, and a half-eaten and highly-suspect granola bar tumbled into the overflowing trash can. She shook her head in a mixture of dismay and disgust. A hank of hair escaped her messy ponytail, and she pushed the offending strands back with an impatient swipe of her hand. A glimmer of gold winked at her from the depths of the drawer catching her eye.

Cam extracted a wire loop holding two tiny keys.

Recognition sparked as she held the keys, letting them dangle from the ring. Her hand plunged into the drawer again, rifling under sheets of yellowed notebook paper.

"Ha!" she cried as her fingers closed around the spines of two more books.

She yanked them from the drawer, a triumphant smile lighting her face when she eyed the tarnished brass locks holding the covers closed. She slid a key into a lock, and her smile gave way to a grin as it popped open.

While she flipped through the pages filled with bubbly pre-teen letters she mumbled under her breath, "Dear Diary, last night I dreamed Veronica's *Alice in Wonderland* doll went all Mad Hatter on the senorita from Spain."

She scanned a few entries, a rueful smile playing on her lips as she relived moments of junior high school angst. She recalled each and every perceived slight, crippling insecurity, and joyful victory with disturbingly vivid clarity. She bit her lip as she skimmed an entry about a devastating lunchroom debacle she was certain would scar her twelve-year-old psyche forever. A name scrawled at the bottom of the tear-splotched page caught her eye.

"Frank," she whispered. She read on, devouring the next few pages in seconds. "Oh my God, Frank." A giggle tripped from her lips, and she lowered the book, scrambling to her feet.

"Hey, Eugene!" Cam shouted over the drone of the drill.

She leapt over a box blocking the doorway and stumbled straight into another shoved against the hallway wall. "Dammit," she muttered as her finger slipped from the page.

"Eugene," she called during the momentary lull in the kitchen.

"No one here by that name," Brad growled.

She plowed through the flotilla of boxes blockading her route to the kitchen and laughed when she pulled up short in the doorway.

Brad squatted in front of the cabinet below the sink, lining his drill bit with the next screw. His paint-spattered jeans gaped at the waist, the elastic band of his boxer briefs proclaiming them property of Calvin Klein. Sweat shimmered on his sun-kissed back. Tiny, damp curls whorled at the nape of his neck as he bent to his task. Two short bursts of power loosened the screw, and it dropped into his waiting palm.

"Good God, you're hot. Way too hot for a guy named Eugene," she commented, lounging against the doorframe and tilting her head as she admired him.

"Still not painting them," he muttered, lining up his next victim. The screw met its fate, and the hinge pulled free. Brad fished a pencil from the back pocket of his jeans, scribbled something on the inside of the door, and set the panel aside.

"We should refinish the doors, maybe have a couple of them fitted with glass fronts, but these are solid maple." He rapped his knuckles against the door. "You can't buy cabinets like this anymore unless you're willing to sacrifice both arms and a leg."

Cam fluttered a hand over her heart. "Oh yeah, talk renovation to me, hot man with power tools," she cooed.

He shot her a stern glare. "Shouldn't you be packing? I think your plan to speed global warming is working. You should be very proud," he added in a dry tone.

He shifted on the balls of his bare feet, turned, and slumped against an unmolested cabinet, dropping onto his ass. His hands dangled from his bent knees, fingers threaded through the drill's cord, dangling the tool against his denim-clad shin. He unfurled his long fingers and the screws he held clattered to the worn linoleum.

"Why am I doing this, again?" he asked, cocking an eyebrow at her.

"Because you like to see me naked," she answered. Cam tossed the forgotten diary onto the cluttered counter and advanced on him like a lion stalking its prey. "And because it moves you one step closer to succeeding in your nefarious plot."

He craned his neck, peering up at her curiously. "Nefarious plot?"

"You can store this stuff in my garage," she quoted in a mocking tone. Cam dropped to her knees, bracing her hands on his. She parted his knees and leaned in. In a low, seductive tone she whispered, "No sense in renting a storage unit. It's a waste of money."

"Trying to be helpful is nefarious?"

"You're trying to lure me into your suburban web by holding my stuff hostage. I might own a mini-storage place for all you know," she taunted.

The drill dropped to the floor with a dull thud. He reached up, capturing her face between large, callused hands. "It's not you I'm after, it's the sub shop."

She trailed one finger down the center of his damp chest, staring at the smattering of freckles dotting the broad expanse of his shoulders. "I knew it. It's hard being an heiress. I just want someone to want me for my body."

Brad pulled her to him and brushed her lips with his. "Added bonus."

Her tongue darted out to wet the spot where his breath tickled her lips. He pushed away from the cabinet, his hands sliding into her hair and freeing it from the bonds of an ancient scrunchie as he claimed her mouth in a breath-stealing kiss.

"Refinish and reface," he whispered when he pulled back.

Cam smiled and lowered her mouth to his shoulder, licking and lapping at the salty sweat coating those delicious freckles while his hands slid through the length of her hair. "Convince me," she challenged.

He barked a laugh and patted her smartly on her bottom. "At this rate we'll never get anything done."

She smiled when she heard the telltale rasp in his voice, her lips curving against his warm flesh. She took a playful nip at his collarbone then murmured, "No hurry. Not going anywhere."

His hands curled around her ribcage, the blunt tips of his fingers pressing into her back. "Oh yes, we are," he stated firmly, pushing her away. "You said you would."

Cam rocked back on her heels and pushed her hair from her face. "I don't want to go car shopping," she muttered, wincing at the petulant note in her voice.

"That was the deal. I help you here, and you give the hunk of junk to the nice man with the car cruncher," he reminded her. "You can trade the Buick, too."

A sudden spurt of annoyance set her teeth on edge. "Why does my car bother you so much?"

Unperturbed, Brad shrugged. "Aside from being aesthetically offensive? It bothers me because the thing is not safe." He reached out and traced the line of her clenched jaw with his index finger, tipping her chin so their eyes met. "I need you safe."

"Thought you didn't like safe."

"There's safe, and there's stupid, and you're not stupid," he retorted. "That thing is gonna break down someplace bad, and I might not be able to get to you."

"So I have to buy a new car so you don't have to play Lancelot?"

A wicked smile creased his face. "No, I still want to play Lancelot," he said with a playful leer. "I just don't want to have to worry about the Black Knight hacking you to pieces along the side of the road."

"You paint such a pretty picture."

"You're too beautiful to drive such an ugly car." Brad punctuated his statement with a kiss, then gave the dismantled cabinetry a meaningful glance. "Do we still have a deal, or do I walk?"

Cam checked the time on the microwave. "Fine. Two more hours and then I let you kick some tires, but I'm not promising anything." She stood, tugging at the hem of her shorts as she surveyed the wreckage of her kitchen. "You'd better be worth all this."

He laughed, and she turned on her heel, prepared to stomp back to her room like a disgruntled teenager. Then she spotted the diary.

"Oh!" She lunged for the counter then waved the book in the air with a smug smile. "I was going to show you this."

Brad stared at the cover of the diary and rolled to his knees. "You've decided to go Anime with Peter?" he asked, plucking the scattered screws from the floor one by one.

"Huh?" She frowned, glaring at Hello Kitty's cheerful face. "Oh. No, no, no. This is my diary," she explained. She fanned the pages with her thumb, trying to regain the spot she'd lost in her journey through the cardboard jungle. "Can you draw Anime?"

"I can draw anything," he answered without a hint of conceit.

"Hmm. Your confidence is insanely sexy." She turned two more pages then grinned. "There. I found your friend, Frank."

Brad's head jerked up. "Frank?"

"Yeah." Cam pressed her finger to the name she'd found. "Frank. I forgot all about Frank," she mumbled. "Here he is."

She extended the book to him. When he hesitated, she smiled and gave an encouraging nod. "It's okay. Just don't pay any attention to the rambling rant about Marcie Johnson and her ginormous boobs. I'm a very jealous woman."

Brad reached for the diary, looking at her warily. Cam tapped her toe while he read, nodding as he slipped one finger under the page and glanced up for permission. "Keep going."

He glanced at her a minute later and shook his head. "Who was this kid, and why was he in your bedroom?"

"Frank. He was Frank," she said, squatting in front of him. "I used to dream about him, you know, after my mom died. I guess you could say he was my imaginary friend."

"Imaginary friend?"

Cam rolled her eyes. "I'm not crazy. Lots of kids have them. Veronica Kelly was convinced some girl called 'Viola' lived in her closet."

"Yeah, I understand the concept," he said impatiently. "Your little friend was a guy who lived in a light bulb?"

Cam laughed. "Okay, maybe a little crazy, but yes." She smiled and reached for the diary. Cam ran one finger over the indentions her pen had left behind long ago. "We fought a lot."

"You and Frank?"

She nodded, a blush rising in her cheeks as she peeked at Brad from under her eyelashes. "My dad and I never fought. I guess we were too afraid of hurting each other's feelings."

"I see," he murmured, tucking her hair behind her ear.

Cam smiled as she met his gaze. "So I fought with Frank." She shrugged and chuckled. "You would have liked him; he had a thing for cars too."

"I think most guys do at some point."

With a devilish grin she confided, "I used to pretend he had a thing for me too."

"I can't imagine how a guy wouldn't," he replied soberly.

"No?"

His smile started slow but grew sure. "I might like you more than my car."

"Wow," she breathed.

Brad nodded, confirming the portent of the sentiment. "My sister called a little bit ago. My parents are coming in next month. I want you to meet them."

Her heart began to pitter-patter. A foolish, sappy grin she couldn't hide made her cheekbones ache. "I've met them," she reminded him.

He wound a lock of her hair around his finger, letting the captive wave unspool at a leisurely pace. "I want you to meet them, Cam," he repeated gruffly. Brad's grass-green eyes bore into hers, clear and determined. "This is all part of my nefarious plot."

Chapter Twenty-Five

Cam bounded down the steps, her sneakered feet beating against the walkway leading from Brad's front door. She cut across the lawn and grinned when she spotted Brad in the midst of a tussle with a little blonde girl over the handle of a red Radio Flyer wagon.

"Do I want to know what you're doing?" she called as she approached.

Brad shot the little girl an exasperated glare, and the spunky sprite crossed her arms over her narrow chest. "I gave Kylie five bucks to borrow her wagon." He turned a fierce scowl in Kylie's direction and growled, "Does your mom know you crossed the street?"

"She knows I'm with you. She watched me cross," she retorted, keeping an eagle eye on the loaded wagon.

Cam bit back a laugh and schooled her features. "What's the problem?"

"She says I'm not *driving* the thing right," Brad answered, rolling his eyes.

"You're gonna break the handle," Kylie complained.

"I am not! This is what the handle is for," Brad argued.

"You're pulling too hard!"

"It's heavy!"

The little girl's blonde pigtails slapped her flushed cheeks as she shook her head. "Let me pull," Kylie demanded imperiously, and Cam lost her hold on the laugh.

She patted the little girl's head. "Sweetie, let him pull the wagon. It makes him feel big and strong."

Kylie craned her neck and squinted up at Brad. "He *is* big."

Cam squatted to look the girl in the eye. "The strong part is what he's worried about," she said in a conspiratorial whisper. Kylie blinked in confusion. "You don't want him to cry, do you?"

Kylie blinked like an owl. "No," she answered at last.

"I promise I'll make him bring your wagon back in one piece. If he breaks it, he'll buy you a new one," Cam told her, shooting Brad a stern glance.

Brad drew a deep breath through his nose, his lips thinning into a line as he rolled his eyes. Cam straightened, tossing her hair back with one hand and reaching for Kylie with the other. "I'll walk you back across the street."

She smiled at Brad. "Stay put until I come back to supervise."

Kylie kept her head turned, her eyes glued on Brad as she and Cam crossed to the safety of her own yard.

"Stay here, and I'll make him give you another dollar," Cam promised.

"How?"

Cam favored the little girl with a dazzling smile then turned and shared its wattage with the tall man clutching a wagon handle across the street. "Honey, I can make him do anything. Stay put," she warned, backing toward the curb then whirling to dash across the street.

"I'm not gonna break her wagon," Brad grumbled as she stepped onto the curb.

"You wouldn't dare, or I'd have to fix yours," she teased. Glancing at the tools and teetering boxes crammed into the wagon, she sighed. "Is this the last of it?"

"Yeah. I got tired of running back and forth."

The corners of her mouth twitched. "I thought you liked running?"

She brushed her hair back from her forehead and caught the twinkle in his eye when the sunlight shot through the sparkling diamond on her finger. He captured her hand, pulling it to his lips and brushing a kiss to the knuckle above the ring he'd slipped on her finger the week before.

"Proud of yourself, aren't you?" she asked.

"Incredibly."

"Well, suck it up, big guy, your sister called."

Brad shot her a wary look. "Which one?"

"Laura. She said your mother is driving her crazy, and everyone will be over for dinner. Apparently, your mom and Steph bought every bridal magazine known to man," she said with a wry smile.

Brad chuckled. "You get the kitchen, Dad and I call the living room. Playoffs start tonight." He stooped to peck a firm kiss to her lips. "That's the last decision I'm making about this wedding. Good luck."

Cam answered with an unladylike snort. "I think your mom mentioned something about pink cummerbunds—"

"No. No pink. No cummerbunds at all," he interjected.

She smiled, standing on tiptoe as she pulled him down for a kiss. "I guess you have more decisions to make." Cam spun on her heel and started toward her father's house.

"Where are you going? I told you this was the last load," he called after her.

She raised one hand in a wave. "Be home in a minute," she called without turning around. Brad grunted, jerking the wagon's handle. "Don't break the wagon."

She trotted across the freshly-cut lawn, checking her father's prized flowerbeds with a critical eye. Cam paused on the bottom step and flipped her hair over her shoulder as she bent to sniff a stargazer lily, her gaze sweeping the yard when she straightened.

Multi-colored balloons tethered to the 'Open House' sign the realtor had planted in the front lawn danced in the breeze. A pair of mockingbirds dodged and darted in and out of the neatly trimmed shrubs. With a surreptitious peek over her shoulder, she furtively snapped one of the fragrant blooms from its stem and carried the lily with her to the porch.

She pushed through the front door and slid to a stop in the foyer, her hand tightening on the doorknob. The house stood empty, stripped of memories and devoid of life. In the center of the living room she turned in a slow circle, mentally putting each chair, table, and unused ashtray back into place.

In the kitchen, she ran her fingertips over the smooth varnish of the newly refinished cabinets and tapped her nails on the frosted glass fronts. Cam spied a paper napkin tucked against the baseboard and swooped to scoop the scrap up. As she crumpled it, a flash of red caught her eye.

She unfolded the napkin, smiling at the sketch of Peter Pincer drawn in the red ink of ballpoint pen. Cam checked the other drawers, recovering the red pen, a stack of take-out napkins, and a screwdriver left behind. After tucking the flower into her hair and shoving the pen and napkins into her back pocket, she tapped the handle of the screwdriver against her palm while she patrolled each room inspecting closets and drawers.

When she got to her bedroom, she stood in the doorway, mesmerized by the tiny vines of rosebuds climbing the walls.

"I'm getting married," she whispered to the empty room.

She stepped inside, her gaze traveling over the bare walls, imagining every picture, poster, and memento she'd ever tacked to them back where they belonged. "To Brad," she continued. "You liked Brad, didn't you, Daddy?"

Cam moved to the opposite wall and stroked the cool, smooth metal of the wall sconce. A sad smile curved her lips. "He's more handsome than Lord Earsamore, Mommy, but every bit as gallant."

A hazy rush of memories made her fingers close around the switch. The worn, ridged metal rasped against her skin. A pool of golden light formed on the glossy surface of the newly polished wood floor. A pair of worn work boots appeared in the very center of the circle and misty dreams morphed into memories and memory solidified in reality.

Cam blinked. A ghost of a smile twitched her lips. "Hello, Frank."

He inclined his shaved head in acknowledgement but said nothing.

"I thought I dreamed you." She tapped the handle of the screwdriver against her palm, offering him a tremulous smile.

Frank said nothing. He stood rooted to the spot in the center of the room staring at her as if he thought she was a dream too.

"I bought a new car. A Honda. Red. Good gas mileage, a CD player. Very safe, lots of airbags... Wait, you don't know about airbags," she babbled.

Frank's eyebrow twitched but he remained silent.

"I'm getting married," she said breathlessly.

He took a step closer to her and extended his hand, palm up. Cam placed her hand in his, marveling at the blue-white light shimmering on his skin. He pulled her hand to his lips and brushed a kiss to her knuckle above Brad's ring.

"Happy?" he asked, his voice rough and rusty from disuse.

"So happy."

Frank smiled, the flash of his white teeth nearly blinding her. Cam jerked her hand back to shield her eyes. Then she noticed the screwdriver clutched in her hand. Her gaze strayed from Frank to the light fixture then sharply back to Frank.

His eyes narrowed with suspicion. "What are you doing with that?"

Cam smiled. "What do you think?"

"Do you even know how to use it?" he snarled.

She snorted. "It's a screwdriver, Frank, not a laser scalpel."

He started toward her as she eyed the wall sconce speculatively. "What do you think you're doing?"

Cam raised screwdriver, gripping the handle in her fist. "I can't just leave you here."

"Don't touch that. You have to turn the power off before you go sticking a screwdriver in electrical sockets."

Cam nodded slowly and lowered her arm. Cocking her head, she peered at him, tapping the translucent orange handle against her thigh.

"What do you say, Frank? You staying here, or do you want to come with us?"

THE END

Margaret Ethridge

Margaret Ethridge survived the tyranny of six older siblings and the rigors of twelve years of Catholic schools, so she can handle anything. A graduate of Illinois State University, Margaret migrated to Chicago where she tried on careers like shoes while attempting to figure out a way to make a living as a professional spinster. Then, she met a Southern man with a sexy drawl and big chocolate brown eyes and her career plan went down the tubes.

Now she lives in Arkansas with that same sweet-talking Southern gentleman. She is the not-so-wicked-step-mother to their two children, the adoring mistress of three spoiled dogs, the food purveyor to eleven hungry goldfish, and the comic foil for one rather impertinent house rabbit who thinks he rules the roost. She spends her days buying booze by the truckload, but at night she spins tales of love and lust.

Margaret is a member of the Romance Writers of America and the Diamond State Romance Authors. When she isn't tapping away at her keyboard, Margaret engages in an epic battle against her never-ending laundry hampers, cajoles the flowers in her yard, sings into her hairbrush, and has been known to hold entire conversations speaking only in movie quotes.

Available now from Turquoise Morning Press
'Concourse Christmas'

A short story in the
Believe: Christmas Short Story Anthology 2010

An unexpected snowstorm leaves Ellie Nichols and Jack Rudolph stranded in St. Louis' Lambert International Airport. What better way to spend a lonely Christmas Eve than getting to know an attractive stranger?

Watch for more of Jack and Ellie's story at
www.margaretethridge.com
and in the upcoming Turquoise Morning Press
Valentine's Day short story anthology!

Coming June 2011
from Turquoise Morning Press

Contentment
by Margaret Ethridge

The debut novel in the Turquoise Morning Press
After Happily Ever line

Tracy Sullivan seems to have it all, a handsome, devoted husband, three beautiful children, a steady career, and the perfect suburban home; but she isn't happy.

The petty resentments that have built over fifteen years of marriage surface when Tracy tells her husband, Sean, that she is no longer interested in sex, and their marriage threatens to implode.

For the sake of their children, Tracy and Sean agree to lead separate lives under the same roof. With the help of a healthy dose of adult-rated fiction and some gentle prodding from a good friend, Tracy begins to rediscover who she is, what she wants, and the reasons she fell for Sean once upon a time.

After two years of soul-searching, Tracy is finally ready to embrace her happily ever after having learned that while happiness may be fleeting, contentment can last a lifetime.

Excerpt from *Contentment*

June 2008

The cursor blinked, the little bastard. The flashing line taunted her, all but double-dog daring her to click the link. But there was someone on the other end. Someone who had seemingly nothing and absolutely everything to do with what may or may not be about to happen. Somewhere out there, caught in the World Wide Web, was a living, breathing person she had never met, never seen, and never heard of Tracy Sullivan.

Tracy glared at the cursor.

Shouldn't someone know they had this much of an impact on another human being? Doesn't she deserve to know what she does matters to someone?

At least, she assumed the author was a woman. Only a woman would understand.

She pressed on the button, and a strange sense of calm flooded her veins as the contact form appeared. After entering her email address, she typed, 'Your stories' in the subject line. Then she chickened out.

Tracy wasn't surprised. She'd been clucking like a crazed hen all day. *I wonder if I'm sprouting feathers yet.*

Out of the corner of her eye, Tracy spotted the telltale pink shopping bag peeking out from under the briefcase she'd had dumped on the chair. She stared at the tiny pink bag, gnawing her bottom lip and remembering the agonizing forty-five minutes she had spent surrounded by a sea of lace and satin.

She stuck out like a sore thumb in the Pepto-Bismol pink store. Her navy blue skirt and peep-toe pumps seemed like such good choices that morning. The skirt may have been navy, but it fit lean and snug. The hem fell below her knee and making her feel like a sexy secretary. She'd paired the skirt with a deceptively simple, white cotton blouse that nipped in at the right spots, and finished the ensemble with the sinfully red high-heeled pumps and a slash of scarlet lipstick. The whole combination had almost given Sean whiplash as she rushed to the car to run the morning carpool shift.

The clucking began. Whatever confidence Tracy had when she dashed out the door fled the moment the whipcord thin, I'm-barely-old-enough-to-order-a-drink salesclerk starting pulling baby dolls and teddies and negligees from the racks.

Tracy gawked at the displays, trying to envision prying her body into one of the scraps of fabric without benefit of a crowbar. She caught a glimpse of herself in one of the store's many mirrors, and her heart sank. She looked exactly like what she was: an almost forty-year-old woman buying lingerie in a desperate attempt to salvage her failing marriage.

Tracy could almost hear the overgrown teenager thinking she'd have to exert some serious effort if she thought she wanted to lure her man back into the nest. These girls probably dealt with a lot of this. Every day, women her age must rush through their door in a blind panic hoping to recapture their youth, and rifling through the inventory of flame red lingerie. Women who wonder if they can tolerate wearing a piece string splitting her ass, on the off chance the butt floss might rekindle a spark.

When this same eager, young saleswoman dared to hold a teeny-tiny bustier set in front of her own non-existent bosom, a woman browsing a rack of full-support brassieres muttered, "Nurse a coupla kids, sweetie," under her breath.

Tracy chuckled, but the clucking began in earnest. The idea of teddies, baby dolls and bustiers had to be jettisoned. She wasn't sure her plan would work. If it didn't, she didn't want to be the idiot flipping flapjacks like Eva Gabor in her high-heeled, marabou-trimmed slippers.

She didn't even have a pair of marabou-trimmed slippers.

Tracy snatched the bag from the chair. She padded into the laundry room and extracted her oldest, softest jeans and a long-sleeved t-shirt from the pile waiting to be sorted and put away. She stepped into the tiny powder room, refusing to meet her own gaze in the mirror above the sink.

Being a chicken, Tracy had refused Sean's offer of dinner, pleading a large lunch. She pretended she didn't notice the bewildered confusion in his eyes when she brushed past him and rushed down the steps. She didn't want him to spot the stupid pink bag. A few minutes later she dashed upstairs again. Silent as a ninja, she checked on the kids, steered clear of the kitchen where Sean prepared lunches for the next day, and sought refuge in the basement room that was her lair.

She glanced up, tentatively scanning her reflection for one little scrap of bravado. It wasn't that she didn't want to see him. For the first time in forever, she was dying to see him. But she wasn't ready. She had to think, and lately she hadn't been able to think clearly with Sean nearby.

She needed a plan. Tracy was nothing without a good plan, but once a plan was in place, boy watch out!

She slowly unbuttoned her blouse, but by the time she stripped out of the day's work clothes she still had nothing. She reached into the pink bag and pulled out a matching bra and panty set in a demure, pale peach with cream lace. She had no idea why she had chosen the set. She hated the color orange and all of its derivatives. She hated fake, antique-looking lace. The last thing any woman staring down the barrel of forty needed to put her body into something with the word 'antique' attached.

She shook the seventy-five dollars worth of polyester at her reflection. "I should make you wear this as a punishment, chicken."

Tracy froze. The peach would warm her complexion, the teeny-bopper titty measurer said. She cocked her head, giving the lingerie a speculative once-over. The color *would* go nicely with her eyes. The lace might not be so old lady-ish on a pair of boobs which hadn't gone completely south yet. Tracy peeked at her bosom.

Not bad, only halfway down.

She stripped off the serviceable bra and panties she wore. Biting off the tags, she caught sight of her body in the mirror and wished she hadn't. Once she put the pretty new bra and panties on, though, a flicker of her fickle confidence returned.

Tracy turned from side to side, inspecting what little she could in the oval mirror above the sink. *Not awful.* She shook her boobs into the cups, pressing on the sides of the bra to be sure the girls were being displayed to their best advantage before slipping into her t-shirt and jeans.

She caught sight of her bare feet as she left the bathroom and smiled. Brazen hussy red. That's what Sean used to call the bright red polish she used on her toes. The glossy enamel gave her the boost she needed.

Her poor toes had gone unpolished for too long. She wasn't the girl she used to be, but Tracy was okay with that. Now. At least she was no longer the foolish woman who had almost thrown everything away.

This has gone on for too long.

Tracy drew on the power of the crimson polish. After all, she needed to be brazen. She desperately wanted to be the hussy she had never been.

She hurried to the computer before she could chicken out again. The cursor still winked at her. She glanced at the ceiling. Pots and pans clamored as they were piled in the kitchen sink. The cursor urged her on, flashing its silent, 'Do it. Do It. You want to do it.'

She wrung her hands. The water shut off, and the lilt of the familiar tune Sean always whistled while he wiped the counters carried down the steps. He was almost done. His kitchen would be sparkling clean and ready for another day's battle.

Another day's battle. She straightened her spine. *I can't wait another day.*

Tracy glared at the nagging cursor and bent, ignoring the bite of the snug denim at her waist. She tabbed down to the tiny message window and paused, her fingers hovering above the keys. Biting her lip, she battled back the panic humming low and insistent in her brain and tried to think of the right words to say.

> *From: Tsull1968@gmail.com*
> *Subject: Your stories*
> *Hi! You don't know me. Well, you kind of do, because you have responded to some of my reviews, but you don't really know me. I just wanted to tell you how much I love your stories. They have helped me more than I can ever explain. I read in your author's notes and the messages you post on the boards that you think these are just silly stories you write and post to make people happy—and they do, I am incredibly happy whenever I get an email saying you have updated. But they are so much more. I just wanted to take a minute to thank you. I know you have no idea what I am truly thanking you for, and that's okay. I needed to say thank you. So, thank you. Wish me luck. Tracy*

With a click of her mouse, the message flew off into cyber-space. Tracy stared at the monitor for a moment, wondering if she should wait for a reply.

Maybe if I get one it would be a sign.

But the sign came from above. The dishwasher hummed to life, and Tracy realized she had to do something now.

No more waiting. No more watching. No more sitting at the computer escaping into another couple's world, another couple's bed. This was it. Now or never.

Tracy cringed at the words as they flitted through her head, but she knew they were the truth. She turned her back on the flashing cursor and headed for the stairs. The time had come. Tonight, Tracy Sullivan planned to seduce her husband of seventeen years, and he'd better damn well cooperate.

Thank you!

For reading this book from
Turquoise Morning Press.

We invite you to visit our web site to
learn more about our
quality Trade and eBook selections.

www.turquoisemorningpress.com

Made in the USA
Charleston, SC
05 January 2011